PHOOLSUNGHI

ADVANCE PRAISE FOR THE BOOK

'Based on real life-characters who quickly acquired legendary status, this lyrical novel plays out in a part of Bihar now considered remote, which, in its heyday, was considered the very centre of pulsating life and creativity. The first full-fledged foray into Bhojpuri literature, sensitively translated, we have before us the prospect of the kind of pleasure derived from slowly reading and savouring a tale of love and romance, joy and suffering, but most of all, of celebrating song and music.'

—Vasudha Dalmia, Professor Emerita of Hindi and Modern South-Asian Studies, University of California, Berkley

'*Phoolsunghi*'s greatest triumph lies in bringing the pulsating soul of an artist to life. Gautam Choubey's English translation succeeds in encapsulating the subtleties of the Bhojpuri worldview so endearingly expressed in the original. I hope that this translation draws the mainstream's attention towards the long-neglected language, literature and culture of the Bhojpuri-speaking people of the world.'

—Manoj Bajpayee, two-time recipient of the National Award

'This brilliantly lively first translation of a Bhojpuri novel dramatizes the intertwined lives of characters that never cease to fascinate and surprise us. Led deftly beyond familiar clichés and stereotypes, we experience the layered richness of a fictional world in which the mundane and the magical are unforgettably blended.'

—Jatindra Kumar Nayak, veteran literary critic and translator

'Probably the first book from Bhojpuri to be translated into English, this charming tale captures very well that quintessentially rural territory whose two defining urban poles are Banaras to the west and Calcutta to the east, both of which this novel visits. Charmingly told, the tale has an old-world setting when opium was still the main cash crop, there were no railways, the British and the Indians interacted on a level that became impossible after the "Mutiny", and no zamindar felt complete without his resident *tawaif* (courtesan) who, however, having her heart in the right place, would fall for the local poet. This deftly plotted novel is well served by an apt translation and enhanced by an "Introduction" in which the translator provides a rich background to the Bhojpuri region and its nascent literature.'

—Harish Trivedi, former professor of English, University of Delhi

'After the iconic *Umrao Jaan Ada*, this is by far the greatest novel around the charisma of a nautch girl. Originally in Bhojpuri, *Phoolsunghi* evokes the ineffable mystique and romance of a lost culture which, for all its political and perhaps "moral" incorrectness, has lost none of the poignancy and poetry underlying its platonic eroticism and romance. In Choubey's inspired piece of translation, this popular and modern Bhojpuri classic is reborn as if were an original masterpiece in English, recapturing a significant bit of cultural history. This book alone might serve the cause of Bhojpuri as no political clamour for reclaiming its classical status can.'

—Sumanyu Satpathy, former professor of English,
University of Delhi

'It is only fitting that Pandey Kapil's Bhojpuri novel should trace the careers and adventures of celebrated Bhojpuri folk poet Mahendar Misar and famous singer Dhelabai. Sparkingly translated by Gautam Choubey, it is truly a delight to read and will transport you into a thrilling world of music, poetry, and love against the backdrop of colonial rule, the opium trade and nationalist politics.'

—Francesca Orsini, Professor of Hindi and
South Asian Literatures, SOAS,
University of London

THE FIRST-EVER TRANSLATION *of a*
BHOJPURI NOVEL INTO ENGLISH

PHOOLSUNGHI

PANDEY KAPIL

Translated from the Bhojpuri by
GAUTAM CHOUBEY

PENGUIN

An imprint of Penguin Random House

HAMISH HAMILTON

USA | Canada | UK | Ireland | Australia
New Zealand | India | South Africa | China | Singapore

Hamish Hamilton is part of the Penguin Random House group of companies
whose addresses can be found at global.penguinrandomhouse.com

Published by Penguin Random House India Pvt. Ltd
4th Floor, Capital Tower 1, MG Road,
Gurugram 122 002, Haryana, India

Penguin
Random House
India

First published in Bhojpuri as *Phoolsunghi* by Bhojpuri Sansthan, Patna 1977
Published in Hamish Hamilton by Penguin Random House India 2020

ISBN 9780670095193

Typeset in Adobe Garamond Pro by Manipal Technologies Limited, Manipal
Printed at Replika Press Pvt. Ltd, India

www.penguin.co.in

MIX
Paper from
responsible sources
FSC® C016779

This is a legitimate digitally printed version of the book and therefore might not
have certain extra finishing on the cover.

Preface

I don't have much to say about *Phoolsunghi*. Its plot must not be mistaken for history, events described in the novel aren't historically accurate, and its characters are fictional; this, I wish to clarify. It is beyond doubt that Dhela, Mahendar Misir, Haliwant Sahay and Revel Sahib were real people. However, since no verifiable account of these characters have come to light, their stories remain full of rumours and legends. Emboldened by a bunch of such legends, the plot of this novel has been invented. Nonetheless, its portrayal of a particular period, a certain region and a specific society is indeed correct.

Pandey Kapil
26 January 1977
2 East Garden Road, Patna: 800001

Introduction

Phoolsunghi (1977) is arguably the most loved of all Bhojpuri literary works. A historical novel, it traverses a period of ninety years in colonial India, roughly between 1840s and 1931. The novel's two protagonists, Mahendra Mishra (hereafter, Mahendar Misir, 1886–1946) and Dhelabai (d 1931), have been drawn from real life. The former was one of the most enigmatic folk poets of Bhojpuri and the latter a *tawaif*, who rose to prominence in a militantly patriarchal society of Bihar. The story of Mahendar and Dhelabai remains one of the most celebrated legends of Bihar and it has attracted three other novel-length explorations.[1]

---

[1] Ramnath Pandey's *Mahendar Misir* (1990) and Jauhar Safiybadi's *Poorvi Ke Dhah* (2012) and Anamika's *Dus Dwareka Pinjara* (2007).

Pandey Kapil (1930–2017) is himself often hailed as the protagonist of Bhojpuri literary movement in post-Independence India. His rendition of the story is an empathetic portrayal tawaifs, patrons and the perpetually rootless folk poets. For these reasons, *Phoolsunghi* calls for attention to a sizeable portion of Bhojpuri's literary and folk heritage.

The Story

Haliwant Sahay, an ageing zamindar from Chhapra, gets Dhelabai abducted and holds her captive at the Red Mansion; she had irked him by spurning his advances, and he wanted to avenge an injured pride. It is at the Red Mansion that Dhelabai meets Mahendar Misir and falls in love—with the man and his music, both. However, her love remains unfulfilled, in spite of Mahendar's quiet reciprocation. With time, Dhelabai rises in social esteem, and when Sahay renounces the world, she inherits half of his property. The inheritance leads to a series of crisis, both legal and personal, eventually triggering Mahendar's departure from Chhapra. After a rewarding short stay in Banaras, Mahendar goes to Calcutta, gets involved in a banknote forgery, and upon his return to his ancestral village, gets arrested for his crime. When Dhelabai learns of his arrest, she mounts a gallant legal defence to secure his release from prison, surprising many with her tenacity. However, Mahendar confesses to his crimes and is sentenced to ten years in prison. The two only manage to meet when it is almost too late.

The phoolsunghi or flowerpecker that gives the novel its name is a tiny bird known for its noisy bustle around flower plants. However, if trapped in a cage, it loses its liveliness and withers away quickly. Phoolsunghi, therefore, is a metaphor for free-spirited creatures, striving for survival and meaning beyond their respective cages. There is, of course, the Red Mansion—the physical cage—where Dhelabai lives, locked away from the world of music that she once reigned over. But there are other cages too: gender, morality, wealth and even 'feeling' hearts. These cages trap the characters of *Phoolsunghi* in social roles and obligations they feel inadequate to fulfill, igniting a desire to break free. It is this desire to rescue a trapped-self that drives most of the action in the novel.

The Author

For close to seven decades, Pandey Kapil championed the cause of Bhojpuri with an indefatigable zeal—leading literary associations, editing periodicals and bearing with grace the burden of being a Bhojpuri author, consigned to anonymity outside the Bhojpuri belt. Kapil did everything by himself: from collecting write-ups to editing, and from raising money for publication to carrying copies of his periodicals to the nearest post office.[2] It will be apt to say that the career of Pandey Kapil mirrors the career of Bhojpuri literature.

---

[2]   Bhojouri Sammelan Patrika, Year 28, Vol. 12, December 2018, p 11.

He was born into an affluent Kayasth household in Sheetlapur, a village located in Saran, Bihar. Devotion for art and literature ran deep into his family. His grandfather, Pandey Damodar Sahay 'Kavi Kinkar' (1875–1932), was an acclaimed poet of the Dwivedi era (1893–1918).[3] Sahay had established a Hindi library in his village and named it Hindi Mandir, signifying his devotion to the then fast-growing language. It was here that Kapil spent most of his formative years, reading books and staging plays. His father, Pandey Jagannath Prasad (1905–88), was a distinguished storyteller who wrote in both Hindi and Bhojpuri. Prasad's best remembered work is *Gaon Ghar Tola* (1979), a Bhojpuri novel which narrates the history of Sheetlapur, traversing nearly three centuries from the reign of Emperor Jahangir (1569–1627) to the 1930s. It is widely regarded as the finest specimen of the 'aanchalik' or regional novel in Bhojpuri, in league with Nagarjun's *Balchanma* (1952) and Rahi Masoom Raza's *Aadha Gaon* (1966). Kapil's two younger brothers, P. Chandravinod (b.1935) and Pandey Surendra (b.1945), sculpt, paint and write in Bhojpuri.

Kapil's literary sensibility bore other influences too. His professional engagement with Bihar Rajyabhasha Parishad, which he joined after completing his BA from

---

[3] Named such after Mahavir Prasad Dwivedi (1864–1938), who steered the progress of Hindi language and literature after the era of Bharatendu Harishchandra (1850–1885).

Banaras Hindu University (BHU), brought him in close contact with writers from across India. Besides, the Patna of his youth was an electrifying place for writers and politicians. The coterie of authors, that met everyday at the Janta Hotel, and later at the Coffee House on Jail Road, showered his sensibility with perspectives of all shade—communist, progressive, orthodox and nationalist. With the establishment of Akhil Bharatiya Bhojpuri Sahitya Sammelan in 1973, the group shifted its base to Kapil's residence. Over the years, his house remained an unmissable destination for writers who happened to be in the city, including the likes of Ramdhari Singh Dinkar (1908–1974) and Panishwarnath Renu (1921–77).

He established two major literary forums, both based out of his residence, and served them till his last days. While Bhojpuri Sansthan (est.1970) oversaw the publication of nearly one hundred Bhojpuri works, Akhil Bharatiya Bhojouri Sahitya Sammelan brought together the entire Bhojpuri literati, scattered across India and overseas. As an organizer, he actively promoted young writers, supported efforts to establish Bhojpuri literary bodies throughout India, kept caste-factionalism away, campaigned vigorously to secure official recognition for the language, and strove hard to create a market for Bhojpuri books—one that could compete with the market for Hindi literature.

His journalistic and editorial practices were liberal and accommodative. During his editorship of four major periodicals—*Humkar* (1951–1952), *Ureh* (1971–1980),

Log (1976) and *Bhojpuri Sammelan Patrika* (1980–2001)—
he promoted young voices, introduced new genres in
Bhojpuri and kept a close watch on the direction of the
language movement. Other than *Phoolsunghi*, he composed
ghazals and poems in Bhojpuri, wrote a short memoir, and
translated works from English and Sanskrit. His other
published works include *Bhor Ho Gayel* (1971) *Kah Na
Saki* (1995), *Jeebh Bechari Ka Kahi* (2004), *Vividha* (2011),
Krishnarjun Samwad (Bhojpuri translation of the Bhagvad
Gita, 2015) and *Sans Chalat Jable Rahe* (2017).

Kapil started his career as a Hindi poet, inspired by
the neo-romanticism of Nirala's *Chhayawad*. From 1955
to 1963, he was associated with Bihar Hindi Sahitya
Sammelan, and from 1966–1973, he was the president of
Saran Zila Hindi Sahitya Sammelan. His early works—
Abhaas (1956, a collection of poems in Hindi) and *Ara
Mein Do Maas* (1961, a Hindi translation of John James
Halls' *Two Months in Arrah*)—were fairly well received.
However, he forfeited his prospects as a Hindi author to
take up the cause of Bhojpuri literature, even as many
others, after dabbling with Bhojpuri for a while, turned to
Hindi for greater fame and success.

For all Bhojpuri authors, both established and
aspiring, Hindi literature constitutes the primary fodder
for their literary sensibilities. When Kapil started writing,
Premchand's literary realism was firmly established in
Hindi, embellished further by the psychological-turn
ushered in by Yashpal (1903–1976) and Jainendra Kumar

(1905–1988). By the 1960s, 'Nayi Kahani' or the new story, pioneered by Mohan Rakesh (1925–1972), Rajendra Yadav (1929–2013) and Kamleshwar (1932–2007), had proudly announced its arrival on the literary scene. Their writings dealt with fractured urban life in a rapidly modernizing India, and the conundrums of women trapped therein. At the same time, a radical literary consciousness, fashioned by the experience of Naxalism in Bihar and the magnetism of Jay Prakash Narayan's ideas—something which the Patna-based writers felt more keenly than others—added to the mix. However, having severed its ways with Hindi, Bhojpuri charted its own independent course, focusing more on rural idealism, patriotic reading of regional histories and issues of the village society, particularly marriage and dowry. It developed an idiom that resisted convenient clubbing with any major literary movements in Hindi, Renu's 'aanchalikta' being the only exception. When Bhojpuri novels like Ramnath Pandey's *Bindiya* (first Bhojpuri novel, 1956), Ramprasad Ray's *Tharuhat Ke Babuwaaur Bahuriya* (1962), Jagdish Ojha's *Rahandar Beti* (1966), Chandradhar Pandey's *Charkha Dai* (1997) and *Phoolsunghi* explore questions of women, they do not borrow the themes or motifs from *Nayi Kahani*, nor their narrative style that focuses on a character's interiority. This was necessary too; at a time when Hindi literature had shifted its settings to urban India, abandoning the villages, Bhojpuri writers continued to deal with the anxieties and aspiration of rural society.

Although *Phoolsunghi* was written and published during the days of Emergency (1975–77), we do not see any major social conflicts, other than those of inheritance, broached in the novel. Instead, the work celebrates the deep emotional ties, empathy and camaraderie between the most unlikeliest of allies; between an ageing English opium agent and a young Indian orphan, between a *memsahib* and the natives; between a concubine-turned-wife and her aristocratic abductor; between an artless prostitute habituated to drinking and a Brahmin music maestro; between a paralysed tawaif, left to beg on the streets of Calcutta, and the man she had once insulted; between lovers who never confront their own feelings, never get intimate. The novel revels in its ability to portray these instances of affective intimacy and man's capacity for compassion. Of course, Haliwant Sahay schemes to press the gullible Doms into his service, but it isn't depicted as an exploitative arrangement; over the years, Bulakna grows to become an important member of the household, eventually earning enough money to start a promising new life in Calcutta. It must be emphasized that Kapil's refusal to delve into the socio-political turmoil does not mirror the general mood of Bhojpuri literature of the time; it was a period of intense creative ferment and politically astute writings. For example, Chaudhary Kanhaiya Prasad Singh's *Geet Jingi Ke* (1978), published a year after *Phoolsunghi,* attempts to rewrite stories from the Ramayana to capture the somber shades of the agrarian crisis, unemployment and class antagonism in Bihar. But Pandey Kapil had other ideas; he chose literary activism, staying clear of realpolitik.

The Folk Poet

Scholars believe that Mahendar Misir was born on 16 March 1886 in Mishrawaliya, a village near Chhapra. However, many others dispute the date, citing an almost twenty-year age gap between him and Bhikhari Thakur (1887–1971), the legendary Bhojpuri folk artist. But this is just one of the many uncertainties surrounding his life— one that has all the substance of a cliffhanger. Even so, stories about his life, conflicting as they are, have a few elements in common too. His platonic relationship with Dhelabai; his arrest for note forgery; Dhelabai's attempt to save him: every account acknowledges these rudiments. Disagreements arise around motives ascribed to his actions. These motives, in turn, determine his public image. For example, stories that suggest he took to forgery to sabotage British economy celebrate him as an unsung revolutionary. By contrast, accounts like *Phoolsunghi*, which attribute the scam to his innocent wish to help courtesans in distress, depict him as an empathetic poet with strong urges, but not too keen to find a larger purpose in life.

Growing up in Mishrawaliya, Mahendar was smitten with wrestlers and storytellers who flocked to a gymnasium near the village temple. The fascination often kept him away from the local school and the Sanskrit literature taught therein.[4] His poetry, as a result, has only vague imprints of Sanskrit poetics; his verses echo popular themes and motifs culled from Kabir, Dharnidas and Lakshmi Sakhi—the saint-poets admired across the Bhojpuri belt. His years of creative spurt coincide with two major phases of Hindi literature: Premchand-led literary realism and the experimentalism of *Chhayawad,* both gushing with nationalist sentiments. Even in the Bhojpuri world, popular poems of Raghuveer Narayan (1884–1955) and the plays of Rahul Sankrityayan (1893–1963) expressed strong anti-British sentiments. Yet, only a single poem in Mahendar's copious repertoire is explicitly anti-British.[5] Is this proof enough that he wasn't a revolutionary? I'll return to that question later.

In the accounts of his life, his relationship with Bhikhari Thakur is often a point of controversy; some project him as a guru-like figure to Thakur, advising the latter on ways to 'elevate' his art, while others reject this version and try to belittle Misir's poetry. It must be emphasized that these disputes are often driven by extra-artistic concerns such as reputability and caste-antagonism. Ironically, neither Misir nor Thakur echo these sentiments. To many, Misir's association with tawaifs and his indictment in forgery are

---

[4] See Suresh Kumar Mishra. 2012. *Mahendra Mishra Ki Pratinidhi Kavitayen.* Mekhla Prakashna: Delhi, p8.

[5] *Humra neeko na lage Ram, goran ke karani* (I do not quite like O Ram, the deeds of the British). Quoted in Dharmendra Sushant. 2019. '*Mahendar Misir: Lat Uljhi Suljha Ja Balam*' Raj: Chhapra.

crimes too grave for pardon. Yet, the songs of Mahendar Misir, which speak of love, longing, migration and faith, made him a household name among Bhojpuri speakers.

The Tawaif

The musical world of *Phoolsunghi* is sustained by a culture of candid interactions among patrons, tawaifs and maestros, each having a well-defined role. Although gurus like Najju Khan, Ramnarayan Misir and Mahendar function as grand patriarchs, the novel is effusive in its praise for the musical abilities of tawaifs such as Dhelabai and Vidyadharibai.

From the mid-sixteenth to the early twentieth century, tawaifs embodied the refinement and sophistication of India's courtly culture. They thrived on the largess of the nobility, and catered to their leisure, excelling in music, dance and literature. As custodians of culture, they commanded both admiration and affection, albeit with the label of 'fallen women.' Stories abound of lovesick admirers raining generosity on their favorite tawaifs, often to the point of self-ruin. *Phoolsunghi* itself begins with a reference to a patron of Janki Bai (1880–1934), who had squandered all his fortune on her mujras.

Unsurprisingly, they were seen as a threat to the idea of family. With the decline of nobility, they were left to fend for themselves, many falling to prostitution. This was also the time when the tawaifs started clearing out of Lucknow and Patna, crowding places like Muzaffarpur's Chaturbhuj

Sthan. The story of Dhelabai's mother, Meenabai, narrated towards the end of *Phoolsunghi*, mirrors this trajectory. The migrant tawaifs brought along art forms popular in the Durbars of Delhi and Lucknow. According to some accounts, a troupe of Iranian-origin courtesans that travelled from Delhi to Lucknow, arriving finally at the court of Hathwa Maharaj in Goplagunj (Saran Division), were the pioneers of Bhojpuri folk theatre. Two of the tawaifs from the troupe, Sudari Bai and Duniya Bai, earned tremendous fame as 'nautanki' artists around 1850s, inspiring others to undertake playwriting in Bhojpuri.[6]

With the rise of scholarly classical singers like Vishnu Narayan Bhatkhande (1860–1936) and Vishnu Digambar Pauluskar (1872–1931), who undertook the monumental exercise of defining, documenting and ordering styles in Indian classical music, the contributions of tawaifs was mostly overlooked. Bhatkhande and Pauluskar established public-funded music schools, taking it outside the system of feudal patronage, and imbued it with a distinct religio-nationalist tone. Naturally, these maneuvers were detrimental to styles like thumri which the tawaifs had invented and perfected.[7]

---

[6] See Jaikant Sing. 2013. *Bhojpuri Gadya Sahitya: Swaroop, Samagri, Samalochna.* Rajarshri Prakashan, Muzaffarpur. p 67.

[7] See Janki Bakhle. *Two Men and Music: Nationalism and the making of an Indian Classical Tradition.* Permanent Black: New Delhi, *The Other Song* (2009). Dir. Saba Dewan.

Throughout the nationalist movement, whenever
the question of the tawaif was broached by writers and
reformers alike, they were discussed as a corrupting surplus,
their tremendous contribution to the progress of Indian
music and dance elided. The idea of reform demanded
a 'post-rescue' life dedicated to renunciation and social
service. However, even a cursory glance at the paradigms
of reform reveals a distinct pattern that aims to dislocate
tawaifs from the centre to the periphery, both spatially and
culturally. At the turn of the century, when the principals
of Patna College and B.N. College urged the authorities
to remove nautch-houses from the vicinity of educational
institutions in Patna, it soon snowballed into a statewide
demand. In Premchand's *Sevasadan* (1919), a drive by
the Varanasi municipality to banish tawaifs from the city
triggers the central crisis of the plot. The beleaguered
protagonist eventually finds refuge as the head of a care
home for children of former courtesans.

Chhapra itself was home to a sizeable tawaif
community who inhabited a block named Shiv Bazaar,
adjacent to the Bhagwan Bazaar. However, a few decades
after Independence, they were driven out of the city. The
temple built by Dhelabai, where Mahendar Misir spent the
final years of his life after serving a seven-year sentence, is
no longer remembered as Dhelabai's temple; it now has a
generic name—*shivaiay* or the home of Shiva. However,
the story of Dhelabai, particularly the way Pandey Kapil
narrates it, offers a different paradigm of rescue: the tawaif

becomes an heiress, moving from the periphery to the centre. She isn't required to repent, but is bestowed with wifehood and awarded a final reunion with her lover.

The Patriots, Sahibs and Migrants

Saran Division is an administrative unit comprising three districts of Bihar: Chhapra, Sivan and Gopalganj. The district of Chhapra, also known as Saran, has its headquarters in the Chhapra City.[8] Saran Division has long been the center of Bhojpuri language movement. It has produced several Bhojpuri authors, including the celebrated trio of Mahendar Misir, Raghuveer Narayan (1884–1955) and Bhikhari Thakur (1887–1971).[9] It is also the birthplace of two of India's greatest political icons—Rajendra Prasad (1884–1963) and Jay Prakash Narayan (or JP, 1902–1979)—something the local populace is extremely proud of. Moreover, during India's freedom struggle, it was a hotbed of armed revolutionaries. If one visits the place, it is easy to see how the air in Saran is laden with tales extolling the exploits of its revolutionary sons; stories about Baikunth Shukla (1910–1934), who avenged Bhagat Singh's hanging by shooting the informant dead;

---

[8] I have used the name Chhapra for the city, Saran for the district, and Saran Division for the larger administrative unit.

[9] Narayan's 'Batohiya' (1911) or the traveler was the most popular anthem of anti-colonial sentiments in the Bhojpuri region, nearly as popular as 'Vande Matram' (1882).

the escapades of Saryoo Prasad (1882–1964), who wrote perhaps the earliest manifestos of revolutionary movement in Bihar. Given the charged political climate of Chhapra during the days of freedom struggle, Mahendar Misir's interaction with revolutionaries seems quite probable, even in the absence of hard evidences; a man so popular among youth must have known, at least, a few revolutionaries, maybe helped them too, as some suggest. Besides, using counterfeited money wasn't uncommon among the underground activists. In 1930, when Yogendra Shukla was arrested from Chhapra, the list of items confiscated during the raid mentions counterfeit coins.[10] Even though the find cannot be attributed to Misir, since he forged only banknotes, the pull of Chhapra's anti-colonial ethos must have been hard to avoid, especially for a folk poet like Misir.

It needs to be emphasized that the land of revolutionaries is the land of Henry Revel or Revel Sahib too. Revel was the custom collector of Chhapra and a much-admired public figure across Saran. Even though he lingers through the novel mostly as a memory, his mystical presence is quite forceful; we see his portrait hung in the prayer room of a Hindu household, and his grave functions as a shrine, which characters frequent

---

[10] See N.M.P. Shrivastava and Jayshri Dutta. 2001. *Aazadi ki Jung: Bihar Ke Mashhoor Krantikari*. Bihar Hindi Granth Akademi: Patna. p 96.

for spiritual succor. It is said that during the final years of his life, he shed his Englishness and roamed the area, helping the locals with money and medicines. Instances of a sahib turning native weren't too uncommon, each transformation having its own peculiar story.[11] According to the eulogy inscribed on his tomb, installed in 1883 at the instructions of the then governor-general of Bengal, the market was named after him in 1788. In the words of Thomas Frank Bignold (1838–1887), the British civil servant who was posted in Patna during the 1860s, Revel was unlike the despotic 'Magistrates of Yore' who ruled with an iron fist:

> Friend to the people, in their midst he moved,
> To all familiar and by all beloved,
> And those who gathered prattling where he came,
> Grey-headed now, still gossip of his name.[12]

Unlike other Bhojpuri-speaking parts of Bihar, Chhapra displayed an attitude of openness towards western influences. The following example is a telling one. Throughout the Bhojpuri belt, English was seen as a threat; there were rumors that education in English was a sinister ploy to Christianize unsuspecting Biharis, and get them

---

[11] See Jonathan Gil Harris. 2015. *The First Firangis.* Aleph: New Delhi.

[12] Anand A. Yang. 1989. The Limited Raj. University of California Press. Berkley. p 92.

deported to Mauritius.[13] However, the general opinion in Chhapra was significantly different. In 1870, when the colonial government decided to withdraw its support to the English medium schools, a meeting was convened in the mofussil to protest the decision.[14] It is highly unlikely that Revel Sahib was alive at the time, yet it is certain that he hadn't faded out of public memory. The eulogy on his tomb is dated 1883, thirteen years after the public gathering in question. One wonders if his bonhomie with the locals was a result of Chhapra's assimilative spirit, or whether he was the force behind the memorandum. It must be highlighted that Saran's cultural syncretism has a long history. With Ghaghara, Ganga and Saryu providing a convenient river-transport network, the area emerged as a major trading center in eighteenth century India, bringing both money and western influences in abundance.[15] Characters in *Phoolsunghi* inherit more than the material assets he has left behind; they live in a world whose moral framework has been set in place by Revel Sahib.

But there were other moral forces at play, too, trying to bring modernity and reform into the region. However, prior to Gandhi's (1865–1948) arrival in 1915, the fate of reform was linked to the fate of reformist organizations

---

[13] See Shreedhar Narayan Pandey. 1975. *Education and Social Changes in Bihar.* Motilal Banarasidass: Varanasi. p 157.

[14] Ibid.

[15] See William Buyers. 1848. *Recollections of Northern India.* John Snow Paternoster Row: London. p 218.

active at the place. The same was true of Bihar. In spite of several proselytizing visits by stalwarts such as Debendranath Tagore (1817-1905) and Keshab Chandra Sen (1838–1884), Brahmo Samaj was a failure. Consequently, the cause it championed the most—female literacy—remained a neglected issue for very long. Arya Samaj, by contrast, made a steady progress, galvanizing members of the lower caste. Between 1872–1873, Dayanand (1824–1883) toured the Bhojpuri belt, lecturing in towns like Arrah, Dumraon and Chhapra. His visit to Chhapra in May 1873 left a lasting impact on the locals. Upon his arrival in the town, he was challenged to a public debate by a certain Pandit Jagannath, a representative of the orthodox Brahmans; as expected, Dayanand prevailed in the debate, boosting the anti-caste voices in the district.[16] Perhaps it is this spirit of Arya Samaj which animates the anti-caste and reformist sentiments in the folk theatres of Rasool Mian and Bhikhari Thakur. Although Haliwant Sahay is no crusader, yet we see a complete disregard of caste and religion-based discriminations in his household; it employs a Muslim cook, a Dom sentry and a butler of indeterminate caste.

For a few chapters in the narrative, the action shifts from Chhapra to Banaras, and then to Calcutta, offering a peek into the world of a Bihari migrant in early twentieth

---

[16] Shreedhar Narayan Pandey. 1975. *Education and Social Changes in Bihar.* Motilal Banarasidass: Varanasi. p 147.

century India. Banaras is part of the extended Bhojpuri belt and therefore not so alien a city. Its vestigial courtly culture comes to Mahendar's rescue, providing him both sustenance and fame. But Calcutta of 1915–1920s, roughly the time when Mahendar lived there, was quite different. The *bhadralok* had mostly outgrown its nineteenth century fascination for courtesans and mujras, glimpses of which can be seen in Bimal Mitra's *Sahib Biwi Golam* (1953) and Sunil Gangopadhyay's *Shei Samay* (1981). In a city that binged on gramophone recordings of Gauhar Jaan (1873–1930)—the diva who reigned the music scene in Calcutta during the period—there must have been no patrician takers for his Bhojpuri lyrics. Naturally, Mahendar is terribly lonesome; the community of fellow migrants is no match for the vibrant social life of Chhapra and Banaras. It is liberating in the sense that it destroys hierarchies of caste, allows characters to escape their past and is capable of some charity, too. However, it is motivated largely by material considerations, leaving a waylaid artist no choice but to return to his village.

To a great extent, the plot is shaped by new 'objects' of modernity, railways being the principal among them. The following lines in Bhojpuri, composed by Ambika Dutt Vyas (around 1858), a Sanskrit teacher at a government school in Chhapra, attest to the wonders of this new world:

Mighty is the reign of queen Vitoria, O Ram,
Throughout the world it stretches, O Hari

Dhuwankas chug away, wherever you see, O Ram,
Telegraph wires are spread everywhere, O Hari.

Dhuwankas or trains play an important role in the narrative. They facilitate Mahendar's escapades, rescue Ramprakash and provide a sense of time, conjuring images of two different historical junctures—before the railroads, and after their development. But the sense of wonder, expressed in Vyas's poem, is not too overwhelming. Characters manipulate these new objects to their advantage; they know their way around the surveillance on a railway platform, print banknotes and use gas lamps in note-forgery.

A note on Bhojpuri

Drawing upon his experience as the series editor for *People's Linguistic Survey of India* (2012), G.N. Devy concluded that 'Bhojpuri has not only stayed alive . . . in the whole world, Bhojpuri is the most rapidly developing language.'[17] According to various estimates, there are close to 200 million Bhojpuri speakers living in India and overseas. While the majority of them live in Poorvanchal—a geographical unit comprising parts of Bihar and Uttar Pradesh—a sizeable Bhojpuri-speaking population lives in Jharkhand, Madhya Pradesh, Chhattisgarh and Nepal. Further, as a result of 'girmitiya'

---

[17] The Times of India (4 August 2017).

or indentured migration during the colonial period (1832–1914), the language is also spoken extensively in Fiji, Mauritius, Suriname, South Africa and parts of the Caribbean. The word Bhojpuri derives its name from Bhojpur, an ancient feudatory located near Arrah in Bihar. The feudatory, in turn, derives its name from Bhoj, the ancient king from Ujjain (Malwa) whose descendants ruled the province.[18]

Literary Bhojpuri claims a fairly old ancestry. It has been suggested that the earliest literary specimen with Bhojpuri expressions date back to the medieval devotional compositions of the Nath sect. The tradition of writing in Bhojpuri begins with Kabir (fifteenth century)—often considered the 'Adi Kavi' or the first poet of Bhojpuri—and includes the devotional compositions of saint-poets such as Dharamdas (sixteenth century), Dharni Das (seventeenth century), Shiv Narayan (eighteenth century), Dariya Sahib (eighteenth century), Lakshmi Sakhi (eighteenth century) and Bulakidas (eighteenth century). By late nineteenth century, Bhojpuri had produced its first literary prose. According to George Abraham Grierson, Ravidutt Shukla's play 'Devakshar Charitra' (1884) is the earliest recorded specimens of literary prose in Bhojpuri. A year later, in 1885, a Banaras based wrestler, Teg Ali, published *Badmash Darpan*, Bhojpuri's first published

---

[18] Krishnadev Upadhyay. 1957. *Bhojpuri aur Uska Sahitya*. Rajkamal: New Delhi. pp 15–16.

work. Yet, a literary culture, so long and diverse, remains largely neglected.[19] If one was to draw a list of factors that may have led to this neglect, two causes stand out: the perception that Bhojpuri is a folk language, spoken by illiterate villagers, and the near absence of its interaction with the other literary cultures, through translations or otherwise. Hopefully, the present translation will change some of that.

Gautam Choubey

---

[19] Udaynarayan Tiwar. 1954. *Bhojpuri Bhasha Aur Sahitya*. Bihar Rashtrabhasha Parishad: Patna p 25.

1

One Life, Two Chance Encounters

Dhela!

Dhela or 'stone' was what she had come to be called. Once, her nautch triggered a violent street fight amongst her fanatic admirers, and in the ensuing mayhem, stones were hurled. That same day, she ceased to be known by her real name and became famous as Dhela.

She was a queen among beauties and an unchallenged sovereign in the realm of music and dance. When the fingers of the accompanist moved briskly over the taut head of the tabla, her skirt swirled like a whirlpool in an ocean. And when mellifluous songs flowed from her lips, it seemed as if her throat was a flute upon which the wind was playing resonant tunes. One could liken her to Menaka, or perhaps to Urvashi, the celestial nymphs. This tawaif from

Muzaffarpur, once the foremost city in the ancient republic of Vaishali, was as majestic as Amrapali—the fabled royal courtesan of that province.

Once upon a time, a famous tawaif called Janakibai lived in Prayagraj. It is said that a devoted admirer of Janakibai was so completely besotted with her songs that he lavished all his wealth on her. However, he had never seen her face, not even a fleeting glimpse, for she always wore a veil. One day, as she absentmindedly lifted her veil and he caught sight of her dark and pockmarked face, he was shocked beyond belief. Could a sound so sweet emerge from a source so repulsive? As his world came crashing down, he exploded with rage and in a fit of uncontrolled fury, stabbed her over and over again. Janakibai miraculously survived the fifty-six stabs and got a colourful new moniker—*Chappan Churi* or fifty-six knives.

Like Chappan Churi, Dhela, too, once had a real name. She was Gulzaribai. True to her name, she was a *gulzar,* a blooming garden of flowers. She was blessed with moonlike radiance and the beauty of a heavenly nymph. But, the deeds of a few fanatics, who clashed over her and engaged in a vicious stone-fight, got her forever renamed to Dhela, alias Dhelabai.

Dhelabai's fame spread-out in all directions just like the rays of the rising sun. When it reached Babu Haliwant Sahay, a powerful zamindar from Chhapra, he rushed to Muzaffarpur to marvel at her splendour. However, when he returned home after meeting her, he was lovelorn and crestfallen. Haliwant Sahay's middle-aged body was home to the soul of a young *rasik*—a devourer of pleasure. Dhelabai's luscious body and her seductive fragrance had filled his heart with unbearable longings and weakened his scruples. Yet, for him, she remained painfully unattainable.

The words that Dhelabai uttered to repulse his advances were steadfast and sacred, like a church bell. But he felt as if they were a dagger plunged into his heart; they had inflicted a wound whose pain pulsated through his veins. She had said, 'Babu Sahib! You must have heard of a *phoolsunghi*—the flowerpecker—yes? It can never be held captive in a cage. It sucks nectar from a flower and then flies on to the next. I come from the community of tawaifs. Members of my community are like a phoolsunghi. Having After sucking money from one pocket, we quickly set out looking for another. Go back home. Spare a thought for your advanced age and spend the remainder of your days saying prayers and chanting the holy name of Lord Ram.'

However, as he descended the steps of her nautch-house, Sahay did not forget to warn her, 'Dhela, my pocket is a limitless fountain of riches. I have no doubt that any phoolsunghi will gladly agree to a life as a captive in my golden cage. Her beak isn't big enough to suck all the nectar from my pocket. And, as to my age, let it be heard that Haliwant Sahay earns his money believing he'll never die. And he lives his life as if he were forever young, like the Ashwinis, the ever-youthful twins of the sun god. It's all right for now. When the time comes, you'll know the hollowness of your own sermon. I am returning home to build a palace for you; a golden-cage for a phoolsunghi. Trapped inside that cage, the flowerpecker will remain perfectly satisfied with a single flower and chirp merrily around it.'

Upon hearing these words, Dhela burst into laughter—a laughter so resonant that it sounded like the harmonized tinkling of a thousand golden bells, all arranged in a long single row. Sweltering under the blaze of that withering laughter, a gloomy Haliwant Sahay retreated to Chhapra.

* * *

Located in Chhapra's Katra colony, his mansion shone as brightly as his *mukhtari*—his career as an official in the law court. But that wasn't all. Besides the mukhtari, there was the zamindari, and in addition to the zamindari, there was the flourishing opium trade.

Sahay shared a bond of deep friendship with Revel Sahib—the opium agent from England—whose carriage ran routinely between Revelgunj and Katra colony. Revel Sahib was a man of exquisite taste. His bungalow was stacked with luxuries from Europe and his cupboard was crammed with a tempting assortment of vintage wines. The sprawling compound in front of his bungalow was bedecked with oak and bottle trees. Its carpet-like grass was mowed with such loving care that one shrank from stepping on it. The red gravelled lane, which originated at the main gate, stretched all the way to the porch. From there, a long series of steps led up to the veranda. The entrance to his bungalow was guarded by a gun-toting guard. A ferocious bulldog, chained next to the door, was always ready to pounce on the intruders and grab them by their neck.

At a little distance from the bungalow was Mukhtar Sahib's office; it was from here that Sahay conducted his business. There was never a dearth of servants and helpers; an army of underlings promptly attended to all of his assignments and personal needs. However, there was no mistress to preside over the affairs of his mansion. Twenty years ago, shortly after giving birth to a son in the twilight of her youth, Sahay's wife and his newborn child had left for their heavenly abode, leaving him bereft in the world. There was enormous social pressure on him to marry again, but Sahay didn't yield to it and decided to live all by himself, just like his English friend Revel Sahib.

* * *

It was as a young opium agent that Revel Sahib had first come to Godna Semariya on the banks of the river Saryu. His beautiful wife found the place to be extremely pleasant and hospitable. The white stretch of sand, on the other side of the Saryu, was dotted with green patches of shrubs and wild grass; it was like a picture painted in white, green and blue. One could always spot a few ferries moored along the riverbank. Loaded with a variety of merchandise, they would sail away to the faraway shores of Rangoon, Singapore and Java-Sumatra. Stationed at Godna Semariya, Revel Sahib would collect raw opium from Gazipur and Balia, and then, dispatch them on boats to the opium factory in Patna. Sahib was always busy with his work. So what was the memsahib supposed to do? How was she expected to pass her time? There was neither a community of fellow Europeans nor a club. Under the circumstances, the memsahib would often venture out alone: sometimes along the river bank, at times aboard a small dinghy, and occasionally, across the river, on to the stretch of silver sand.

As is the case with all commercial towns, life in Revelgunj was always teeming with activity. Often, in the evenings, the sahib was seen taking the memsahib on a hurried carriage ride to Chhapra. The district collector, judge and civil surgeon in Chhapra, all three were British gentlemen. The evening parties with their families provided a little diversion. However, since the memsahib remained childless, she needed more than the occasional get-togethers with a select few to relieve the boredom of living alone in a mofussil. The couple, therefore, started spending time in the company of the locals, hoping earnestly to improve their social life. Once in a while, they would even cross the Saryu to sport-hunt along the small river delta: sometimes hunting a deer, sometimes a wild boar, and at times, just a bird. As the two busied themselves in their daily struggles, time went on surreptitiously. And before they could realize it, they had already spent twenty-five years of their life in the province, forming deep emotional ties with the place. To honour the sahib, the local market was named after him as Revelgunj. Slowly but surely, without consciously striving for it, the two became an integral part of that world.

Life went on at its usual pace until the unthinkable happened; the region was struck by a plague epidemic and the memsahib became one its victims. Chhapra's civil surgeon put in a heroic endeavour to save her and Revel Sahib nursed her as assiduously as a man possibly could, but to no avail. During her final moments, the memsahib had urged her husband to give her a burial in Revelgunj. Even in her death, she did not wish to be separated from the well-wishers and friends in the midst of whom she had lived the best years of her life. Honouring her wish, she was laid to rest on the banks of the Saryu.

The day she was interred, Revel Sahib sobbed for hours at her grave, quite unmindful of the clock. Noon turned to dusk and dusk melted into the night. But could any night rival the deep darkness that his life had plunged into? When the sahib composed himself, he noticed being gently held by a boy of fifteen or sixteen. The boy was trying to help him rise to his feet.

'Sahib, please get up. Let us go home,' the boy requested softly.

'Fool, nothing is left of home.'

But that reassuring touch brought him immense peace and he let the boy guide him to his bungalow.

'Who are you, brother? Are you God's own messenger, an angel?' Revel Sahib had asked.

'I am Haliwant, your new clerk.'

That first exchange of words proved to be a decisive moment for the boy. It was to change his fortunes forever. Soon, the fifty-year-old Revel Sahib befriended the boy of fifteen and a most endearing relationship took root. The boy started mastering the language and the etiquettes of the English, while the sahib started absorbing Indian manners. Gradually, the management of the opium trade fell into Sahay's hands, and the sahib's life began revolving around his medicine box.

In a short time, Sahay's fortunes soared: he got married, took possession of Chhapra's White Mansion, bought off the local zamindari, and through Revel Sahib's good offices, he had the district judge appoint him as a *mukhtar* at the Chhapra law court. But the sahib had not been able to leave Revelgunj even in all this time.

2

A House for the Drifters

Haliwant Sahay's father, Babu Balwant Sahay, was a lower echelon employee of the East India Company and worked at the office of its Delhi Resident. One of Balwant's uncles was also based in Delhi. He worked as a clerk in the Punjab Survey Office. The two were birds of a feather—of the same age and the best of friends. Each year, they availed a leave of two months and travelled together to their native village, riding an *ekka*—a one-horse buggy. Back in those days, the railroads were yet to be laid and Bahadur Shah Zafar, the last of the Mughals, was still the titular head of India. But the real authority had already slipped into the hands of the Company. The journey from Delhi to Sheetlapur, a remote village near Chhapra, was long and perilous. However, since the two were employees of the

Company, they had little fear of the dangers that lurked on the road; their association with the then-unproclaimed rulers of India nearly guaranteed them personal safety, and a few other comforts along the way too.

In the beginning, both their families stayed in the village. However, once Balwant's uncle acquired a little property in Punjab, he decided to take his family along and relocate for good, thus severing all his ties with Sheetlapur. But Balwant had little choice in the matter. For years to come, he had to keep up with this annual sojourn. Later, when he was already along in years, his third wife bore him his first child, Haliwant Sahay.

As one would have expected, Balwant did not live very long to look after his son. The poor boy became fatherless at the tender age of ten. Before any signs of a moustache could appear on his upper lip, his mother, too, had departed for her heavenly abode. The young Haliwant Sahay was placed in the care of an aunt who was brusque and heartless. His cousins added to his woes; they were prickly and impossible to put up with. Feeling unwanted and helpless, he ran away from Sheetlapur and sought refuge with his maternal uncle who lived in Godna Semariya. His maternal relatives—his aunt and uncle— were full of compassion, but practically penniless. With no means to support his nephew, the uncle pleaded with Revel Sahib and found a job for Haliwant Sahay. This is how he became the deputy clerk at the Opium Bungalow. His salary was set at three rupees a month. He found the amount so astronomical that when he got his first salary, he felt like the lord of the three realms.

'Would you be interested in working as a clerk? You are of the Kayasth caste, aren't you?' Revel Sahib had asked.

The bashful fifteen-year-old could merely nod in agreement. In those days, being a Kayasth was one's permit to the clerical profession. It was precisely this caste affiliation that had landed his father a job as an accountant with the East India Company. But Haliwant Sahay wasn't destined to remain a clerk forever. Although he had come to work as one, he ended up becoming Revel Sahib's loyal sentinel, his trusted manager and bosom friend.

* * *

'Haliwant, I'll sculpt a true Englishman out of you and take you to England, as my adopted son. You will come with me, won't you?' Revel Sahib would often announce.

Whenever Revel Sahib made that suggestion, Sahay would merely nod his head to signal his consent. But this repeated declaration of an eventual return was to remain unrealized since the sahib could never tear himself away from Revelgunj. Even though he strove hard to groom Sahay into becoming an Englishman, he himself kept evolving into a Hindustani—an unadulterated specimen of a Bhojpuri-speaking rustic. Sahay's transformation into an English Sahib was a swift one. As he established his grip over the opium trade, coat and trousers became his preferred attire, English became his preferred language and his gait betrayed a lordly disposition typical of a sahib. But Revel Sahib became a shadow of the man from England. Gradually, memories of the distant homeland faded away and he felt like a native of Revelgunj: the local medicine-man, a grandfather to the entire community.

Once, Sahay had tried to remind him gently of his oft-announced plan. 'Sahib, won't the two of us go to England?'

Nudged about his old scheme, Revel Sahib kept staring blankly at Haliwant. Following a few moments of uneasy silence, he replied in jest, 'You Kayasths are so much like the English: a stream of water, that's what you are. Wherever the stream finds a slope, it flows along. It can never be tied down to a place.'

After a moment's reflection, he added, 'Haliwant, you see, this place here, this Revelgunj—this is now my England, my home. And I won't desert it for anything in the world, nor would I let you go anywhere, sailing across the seven seas.'

That day, after a very long time, Revel Sahib put on his English suit, got into his carriage and rode out. By evening, his bungalow was bursting with noisy revellers. Arrangements for what appeared to be a grand celebration were afoot; a confectioner was busy supervising the preparation of local cuisines and traditional sweetmeats. When Sahay returned to the bungalow, after his routine roundup of the opium farm in Chhapra, he froze at the entrance. Nothing of what he saw made sense to him. 'What are these women doing inside Revel Sahib's bungalow?' he gaped and wondered.

Just then, Revel Sahib walked up to him, thumped the unsuspecting youngster on his back and said, 'Get inside, Haliwant. Wrap a new dhoti. Today is your tilak, your engagement.' As he shed light on the occasion, a feeling of triumph was writ large on his face. Before the day ended, Sahay was engaged. His maternal uncle and aunt were beside themselves with joy. 'Now that I have clipped his wings, this birdie won't dream of flying to England,' Revel Sahib had said to himself.

Impulsive though it might have appeared, it wasn't a decision made in haste. Sahib had been mulling it over for quite a while. He knew of a suitable match in Manjhi, the neighbouring village. There was a girl whom he had cured with his medicines the year before. Earlier that day, when he had set out on his carriage, he had gone to Manjhi with a formal proposal for Sahay's marriage. Revel Sahib saw to it that the elaborate rituals were completed within a day, and, by late evening, the entire town of Revelgunj had partaken of the ceremonial feast at his bungalow.

But even after the tilak, dust didn't settle on the sahib's carriage. Soon afterwards, a routine of daily trips from Revelgunj to Chhapra commenced. Every morning, the sahib would embark for Chhapra and return to Revelgunj only by late evening. And before anyone had the time to reflect on the strange monotony of the sahib's enterprise, as he went about making a few secret arrangements, the day of the wedding had already arrived. After all the matrimonial rituals were performed, the palanquin ferrying the young bride set forth for the groom's place. The jubilant entourage was led by Revel Sahib's own carriage; on the carriage sat the groom, with the sahib keeping him company. But when the baraat reached Revelgunj, instead of taking the turn that led to the sahib's bungalow, it marched straight ahead.

'Where are we headed?' a befuddled Haliwant asked.

'Chhapra,' Sahib made a curt reply.

When the entourage reached Sahib's Chhapra bungalow, Haliwant's maternal uncle and aunt were already there. The bride was given a traditional welcome. As soon as she set foot into the house, people queued up to observe the rite of *moohdekhi* or 'behold the bride'. When Revel Sahib's turn came, he blessed her with a most magnanimous wedding gift: having secretly transferred the ownership of his bungalow, assets and other business interests in Chhapra to Sahay, he entrusted his bride with property registration papers. And before returning to Revelgunj, he even surrendered the deeds of his mukhtari to Sahay.

'Haliwant, I want you to stay in Chhapra and come tomorrow, you must start your practice at the district court,' he ordered.

Sahay teared up at the suggestion and protested vehemently, 'No, Sahib, I won't leave you for the sake of a mukhtari, nor will I stay in Chhapra.'

Sahib caressed him lovingly and chuckled at his childlike petulance. 'No, son, there is no getting away from this. You have to manage your mukhtari and stay here in Chhapra.'

That evening, Sahib retuned to Revelgunj, all by himself.

3

The Cage by Saryu

By the time the train stopped at the Chhapra station, it was already dawn. Babu Haliwant Sahay alighted from his compartment, looking careworn and dazed. His clothes were soiled, his hair was scruffy, his cheeks were covered with a grey stubble and his eyes were a little inflamed, for he had not slept a wink the whole night. As soon as he got down, the platform woke up to a sudden excitement. The stationmaster rushed to welcome him, offered his salaam and escorted him away from the platform. Addressing the stationmaster in English, Sahay made a polite request, 'Stationmaster Sahib, I don't think my carriage has arrived yet. Please arrange one for me.'

A carriage was hired and Sahay boarded it at once. But no sooner had it started moving than a thought occurred to him. He was reminded of Revel Sahib and his wise assessment of the human condition: 'Haliwant, man is a puny creature. Only time and circumstances propel him to greatness.' It was so true. Sahay's own high stature was the handiwork of time and circumstances. That day, it was because of those two mysterious forces that he was compelled to return to Chhapra, feeling wretched and powerless; it was because of them that he had to suffer a painful humiliation, that too at the hands of a harlot.

Sahay had witnessed a great many things in his life, and had endured much too. Twenty years ago, while still a young man of thirty-five, he had become a childless widower. By then, Revel Sahib was also dead. Had he been alive, perhaps Sahay wouldn't have decided to lead a solitary life after his wife's death. Revel Sahib had also lost his wife, but it had happened around the onset of his twilight years. He, too, had been childless, but he found a pillar of support in Sahay. It had helped him spend the remainder of his days with a little joy and abundant contentment. Revel Sahib had tasted each wine that life had bestowed on him. Sadly, he could not inspire a similar yearning for the bittersweet gifts of life in Sahay.

Revel Sahib had lived the life of a saint—a life dedicated to serving others. Sahay always looked up to him and idealized his ways. Following his example, Sahay committed himself to an erroneous choice after the death of his wife; moved by Revel Sahib's dedication to his dead wife, he too, decided to spend his days alone. Leaning on

Sahay, Revel Sahib could happily complete his earthly
chores, before retiring to the final union with his maker.
However, Sahay remained trapped in the bog of worldly
concerns. He found no one to stand by his side. As his
influence and prosperity soared, he kept sinking deeper
into that bog. That day, at the age of fifty-five, his edgy
and long-repressed libido was once again on the boil.

* * *

When his vehicle clattered past the turn at the end of
Bhagwan Bazaar, it suffered a sharp jolt. The sudden bump
forced Sahay, presently drooping from fatigue, to look out
of the carriage's window. The stream of the river Saryu
had shrunk and mounds of sand lay sprawled across the
riverbank. A cowherd, who stood by the edge of the road as
his cattle grazed, was engrossed in singing a *poorvi*.

> 'Build me a bungalow, along the sandy swathe,
> O Kishori Lal,
> Where the waves of the river Yamuna would frolic
> and splash.'

'All right, then, it is decided. I, too, shall build such a
bungalow on the sandy riverbank. And the waves of Saryu,
if not of the Yamuna, will splash against it. Don't worry,
Dhela. Let the time come. I understand that man is awfully
feeble. It is also true that only time and circumstances

elevate him to greatness. But both dance to the tune of a man who dares to rise. I will become that man. Why couldn't Revel Sahib, my greatest teacher, my dearest friend, come to embrace this simple truth?' he thought, his languid eyes lit up with hope.

His carriage stopped at the entrance of his mansion. The gatekeeper bowed in salutation and pushed open the heavy iron panels of the gate, with a loud, grating sound. As the carriage drove in, a chained bulldog began barking excitedly, but it grew quiet as soon as it recognized the master. His early morning arrival has set the entire mansion bustling with frenzied activity; nearly a dozen servants scampered about in all directions, trying to bring the mansion to perfect order. Seeing the grandeur of his world, Sahay smiled underneath his bushy moustache.

'Although the house is full, my heart aches with sheer emptiness. This mansion is destined to remain bare, but my heart can no longer endure this void.' Summoning Pataluwa, he said imperiously, 'Pataluwa, go fetch Registrar Sahib immediately.'

The young Rai Lachhman Prasad was a native of Basti district and an empathetic companion to Sahay's youthful heart. During the Sepoy Rebellion, his father, Rai Kamtanath Prasad, had avidly supported the British efforts to quell the uprising and had even held the rank of a subedar in the British army. Kamtanath Prasad's loyalty had earned his son the sub-registrarship of Chhapra. Lachhman Prasad was also a happy recipient of Sahay's largesse, and a friend to all and sundry. As soon as he arrived, Sahay made an impatient request, 'Registrar Sahib, do you see that stretch of land—the one that starts from the south of the bend in the road and goes all the way to the bank of the Saryu? I want it registered in my name by today evening. Whatever money is needed for the job, please ask for it at the house.'

Dumbfounded, Prasad gaped at his friend. Sahay turned towards him, outlined his plan once again and said, 'Registrar Sahib, don't look so shocked. I have to build a bungalow there, so close to the water that the waves of the Saryu could splatter against it. It would be the golden cage where a phoolsunghi could be cradled.'

Leaving Prasad even more clueless than before, Sahay walked away gleefully, towards the inner wing of his mansion. One could hear him sing, in that gruff voice of his.

'Build me a bungalow, along the sandy swathe,
O Kishori Lal,
Where the waves of the Yamuna would frolic and splash.'

* * *

Soon, a palatial house, which would become famous as the Red Mansion, was built on the stretch of land that bordered the riverbank, just as Sahay had envisaged it. And a sprawling lawn bedecked with a selection of plants and trees, indigenous as well as foreign was added to it. A delightful little garden of roses, which was laid out in the middle of the lawn, enhanced its verdant loveliness. The compound's southern wall was fortified to withstand the ebullient waves of the Saryu. A horse stable and a garage were constructed along the western flank of the campus, as were small quarters for gardeners and retainers. A huge iron gate was installed along the eastern wall, and next to it, a cabin for the gatekeeper. The red gravelled path, which ran through the gate of this stately mansion, led all the way to its porch.

One day, while the construction of the Red Mansion was still underway, Prasad had asked, 'Mukhtar Sahib, you already live in such an imposing mansion, why build a second one?'

'Registrar Sahib, you are but a naive village boy. This is no mansion. Hadn't I told you this is a cage? A golden cage to cradle a phoolsunghi,' Sahay had replied, his bushy moustache concealing his enigmatic smile. Prasad was still thoroughly puzzled. Taking pity on his friend, Sahay offered him a cup of wine.

4

A Priceless Gift

A grand jamboree, with Dhelabai as its central attraction, was at its peak. Seth Ramratan Sahu's daughter was getting married and the baraat had already arrived. To entertain the guests, Dhelabai had come all the way from Muzaffarpur. Bewitchingly fulsome physique of a woman in her early twenties, golden radiance and the voice of a cuckoo—such were the features of the angelic Dhelabai. Her nimble feet were like the wings of a butterfly—quivering and soft. And her body was supple, like the tender *koen* plant. But who all were entitled to marvel at the exploits of the magnificent Dhelabai? Who all had access to this elite assembly of the blue-blooded that had come together with the baraat? Not many; this spectacle wasn't for everyone to devour. Several jesters and street performers from Lucknow had been hired to keep the lesser mortals amused.

A colossal marquee, held together by one hundred and twelve poles, was erected in the middle of the inn's courtyard. Right in the middle was a colourful nautch-house, a barricaded area which only the patricians could enter. All around the central arena of that makeshift nautch-house stage, elaborate arrangements were made for the patricians to sit, squat, recline and relish the performance contentedly.

'O' beloved, do not forfeit my reminiscences,' Dhelabai sang.

The perfect harmony between the lovesick lyrics of the *birahin* and the graceful steps of Kathak rained rasa on the entire jamboree. That deluge of emotions swept everyone adrift in a sea of ecstasy. Set against the silence of the standstill night, the celebration overflowed with a dazzling array of songs and astonishing dance acts. Intermittently, the huge four-faced clock, mounted atop the inn's gate, tried to alert the revellers to the passage of time; *tang tung,* it clanged.

* * *

Close to midnight, a little hubbub arose at the gate. Suddenly, the huge iron-gate, that was already ajar, was thrown open completely and advancing footsteps were heard. The menacing noise kept drawing nearer, *ghabad-*

ghabad! The gatekeeper tilted his flickering torch and strained his eyes, trying to make things out in the dark. As the tension escalated, fingers of the tabla player froze in terror, the sarangi's bow got flung aside and Dhelabai's performance came to a sudden stop. Brandishing shiny swords and toting guns, over fifty men had invaded the inn. A thundering voice issued a grim warning to the pleasure-seekers, 'Nobody moves or you will lose your head.'

Moments later, when the petrified revellers looked around the marquee, their eyes wide with dread, they realized that none of them had been harmed in the raid. Some people claimed to have seen a giant elephant swaying at the gate, like a giant shadow, but there were no signs of a robbery. The gang of dacoits had left the venue with the same startling speed with which they had appeared. The entire episode had transpired within the wink of an eye!

But wait, where is Dhelabai? Whatever happened to her?

People were scampering away to the safety of their homes, shaking their heads in disbelief and shock. In the midst of that mayhem, none had the wits to notice that the jamboree had been robbed of its most precious gem. Dhelabai was missing! Within a few moments, the inn bore a deserted look. The fearsome gunmetal cannon, that always stood proudly outside the inn's gate, and was rumoured to have been cast in Iran, waited in silence—purposeless and without anyone to command it.

Built over a century and a half ago, the inn must have sheltered several communities during times of danger;

its formidable iron gate must have withstood numerous attacks and kept the invaders out. On countless occasions, to defend those seeking refuge, the awesome cannon must have roared and spouted flames. About forty years ago, during the Sepoy Rebellion, the same inn had protected all of Chhapra. But that day, it had failed Dhelabai; its high gate was open and the cannon stood cold. The robbers had succeeded in abducting Dhelabai from the midst of a milling crowd.

The raid had laid waste to the grand jamboree and the revellers had retreated to their homes. Only sad reminders of the spectacular party—abandoned tablas, unaccompanied sarangis, smashed cups, forlorn rolling bottles and haphazardly thrown bolsters—lay scattered all over the place. Meenabai stepped out of her tent and looked around, trying to make sense of the bedlam. Moments later, she spotted Dular Khan, the tabla player, presently walking towards her.

'What happened, Dular? What is the matter?' Meenabai asked nervously.

'Oh, Mother! Gulzaribai . . .' Dular Khan wanted to tell her everything but found himself choking.

'What about Gulzaribai? What has happened to my daughter?' By now, Meenabai was on tenterhooks.

'The dacoits took her,' after much struggle, Dular Khan muttered.

At these words, Meenabai let out a piteous cry and ran towards the nautch-house, pounding her breasts at the misery that had befallen her. But, alas, the nautch-house was completely desolate.

* * *

Squatting on the inn's veranda, a little further from the nautch-house, a huddled group of servitors were preparing *khaini* by kneading tobacco and lime on their palm. They spoke lustily of Dhelabai's beauty and her skills. Upon seeing the dacoits, a few among them had leapt to their feet, hoping to challenge the invaders. But sensing their ferocity, even those who dared to rise stood lifelessly in terror. To the great horror of the dumbstruck revellers, the dacoits had simply ambled in, put Dhelabai on an elephant and carried her away, without facing any resistance whatsoever. No one could let out as much as a hushed sound of pity.

Among the servitors sat a young man—a connoisseur of music and a devotee of *birahin* and poorvi. The magnetism of Dhelabai's shining reputation had drawn him out of his village and brought him to the town: from Mishrawaliya to Chhapra. Since his rustic hesitancy had prevented him from entering the nautch-house, he had chosen to squat on the veranda, along with the servitors. Once the dacoits left and the ensuing furore faded into a rambling murmur, he stood up and quietly strolled out of the gate.

* * *

Ram-Ram! Pronouncements of censure and remorse continued well into the dawn. The inn's gate, shut firmly after the ruinous raid, was thrown open once again. Escorted by Dular Khan, Meenabai emerged out of the premises; she appeared downcast and walked barefoot. O where would she look for Gulzaribai? Who will tell the anguished mother of her daughter's whereabouts?

When the *kotwal* saw her weeping, he let out a callous laughter and said, 'What are you crying over, Meenabai? Get over these sentimental attachments. You won't get her back now. It is time to put a price on your daughter. How much money do you want to let this matter be forgotten?'

'Price? What price, Kotwal Sahib? Gems and jewelleries have price tags, but the moon is priceless. Who in this world has the resources to buy my moonlike Gulzaribai, Kotwal Sahib?' Meenabai retorted, her words sharp as an arrow.

Gulzaribai was kept locked inside the Red Mansion. Outside, Meenabai waited in complete silence. She clutched the bars of the gate's grilled window and pressed her face against it, hoping desperately to catch a glimpse of her daughter. Gulab Singh, the fearsome rifle-toting gatekeeper, kept a strict vigil on her. His moustache was warped, as was his tongue. Just then, she heard a voice coming from behind her: 'What is the matter, Meenabai? What do you want?'

As she turned back, she felt completely mesmerized by the sight of that stentorian-voiced man; never before

in her life had she beheld a face so magisterial. His aura
was so overpowering that the lion-like Gulab Singh turned
instantly into a terrified fox and scrambled to open the gate.
Meenabai had seen a great many things in her life; it did
not take her long to realize that the man she stood facing
was none other than Babu Haliwant Sahay Mukhtar.

'Why don't you come inside, Meenabai?' said Sahay, as
he entered the gate.

She obeyed and started following that imperious man,
without uttering a word of protest or plea. They crossed
the lawn, walked past the bed of flowers, reached the steps
to the porch, stepped on the veranda, entered the main
door, and at last, found themselves in the sitting room.
Sahay plopped down on a couch, turned to Meenabai and
came straight to the point, 'Look Meenabai, instead of this
daily niggling, I want you to claim a one-time settlement
for your daughter.'

The worldly-wise Meenabai bowed in salutation and
said, 'Sarkar, I don't want to sell my daughter. How can I
accept a price? Gulzari will be my humble offering at your
feet. What more could a wretched like me present before
you?'

That day, Sahay felt a strange sensation wash over
him. He was instantly reminded of an incident from his
childhood. He remembered the day his father, Balwant
Sahay, had returned to Sheetlapur. He was on leave from
his office in Delhi and had come home riding an ekka,
as he always did. There was a general chatter that at an

auction organized by the Company government, Balwant Sahay had acquired the entire estate that belonged to the zamindars of Manjhi. And since he had become a rajah himself, where was the need to return to his job in Delhi? Those rumours were true. The zamindar's widow had failed to deposit the annual estate-tax and the Company government had put all her land up for auction. When the deeds of auction reached Balwant Sahay at his office in Delhi, he paid up for the ownership of the entire estate to be transferred to him.

The following afternoon, as Balwant Sahay was washing his hands after lunch, a palanquin carrying the zamindar's widow stopped at his doorstep. The widow got down from her palanquin and spoke to him thus: 'You have bought all of my land at the auction and there is nothing that I have to say about it. But, such is my condition, that even a ripe cucumber will soon become too expensive for me. I beg you, with the *aarchal* of my sari spread out in prayer; please, give a little something for me to survive on.'

Haliwant Sahay still remembered every detail of that day. Upon hearing that piteous imploration, his father had disappeared into the house, making a *khatar-khatar* sound with his wooden clogs. A little later, he remereged, carrying the auction papers in hand. 'Sarkar, several generations of my family have lived off your patronage. Bones in my body are sodden with your salt. I haven't bought this to usurp your estate, or to become a rajah myself. I have bought it with the sole intention to protect your zamindari. This has always been yours, please accept it.' With those words, he placed all the deeds into her *khoenchha*.

And today, with the same nonchalance, Meenabai had placed her daughter—a woman more precious than an entire estate—in Sahay's khoenchha.

5

O' Beloved, Remember Me

The young man walked out of the inn and melted away into the darkness. Five or six years ago, when the railroad was being laid and he was still a curious little boy, he had come to Chhapra to marvel at that modern miracle. And that evening, now in the prime of his youth, he had returned to the city, hoping to savour another miracle—the spectacle of Gulzaribai's *mujra*.

The inn's gatekeeper was already scared and shaken. When he saw the young man, he gasped in fear, and, quite unthinkingly, muttered a question he was accustomed to repeating ever so often—'Who goes there?'

'Mahendar Misir.' That was all the young man said, as he sauntered out of the gate. It was difficult to locate anything in that blinding darkness. Only the pond across from the inn sparkled with reflections of the twinkling fireflies that hovered along its edge. At some distance from the inn, near the bend in the road, an elephant swayed away nonchalantly; it looked as eerie as a shape-shifting shadow under a torch. One could also see a group of phantom-like men beetling off on either side of that beast.

For a few moments, an astounded Mahendar merely gawked at the scene. A burning sting raced through his veins as he recalled the song Dhelabai was singing moments before her abduction—'O beloved, forfeit not my reminiscences.' Could he ever get past the memories of that day, he wondered. And then, turning on his heel, he flitted away in the direction opposite to the marching elephant.

Soon, he reached the railroad, his mind still reeling from the shock. He could see the station, the deserted platform and the lonesome glass lamp that flickered atop a pole. As he crossed the tracks, he found himself near a sunken smallholding—the kind where rain water stagnates. However, the summer blaze had rendered it completely dry and its parched bed was full of cracks. In an inexplicable haste, he stomped past the smallholding, crushing paddy stubble under his feet and making a *chur-chur* sound with each hurried step. Every now and then, a hedge intersected his trail; it was only with great vigilance that he avoided stumbling at them. In that impenetrable darkness, whenever he had to navigate past a water divider, he really struggled to keep his balance. But has anyone seen the living walk around in such darkness? Could it be Mahendar Misir's ghost, and not the man himself? He marched on frantically, like a man possessed. Even so, what illuminated his trail, that pathless path? Perhaps his agony was his oarsman. It was perhaps the niggling pain in his heart that burnt like a lamp and lit up everything around him. It was the excruciating burden of remembrance. 'O' beloved, forfeit not my reminiscences.'

The all-embracing darkness was confounding. Cloaked in coarse dark blankets, everything around him stood quiet and motionless; the plants, the trees and the villages that he walked across, each one of them stood side by side, rolled up in an indistinguishable black bolus.

A little later, the birds launched their merry chirp, but the sombre song in his heart lingered on. 'O' beloved, forfeit not my reminiscences.' Finally, after traipsing for hours in blinding darkness, he saw the first light of the dawn—a gentle hue of red—flash on the horizon. But wait, what is this place that he has arrived at? What village could it be? No, this is not Mishrawaliya. Oh, this is Pakadi, the maestro's village. And that house ahead of him belongs to the master himself. Stunned by the outcome of his night-long meanderings, Mahendar stood transfixed at the doorway of Pandit Ramnarayan Misir's residence; somehow, the distressed soul had turned up at his guru's house. As he waited outside, he could listen to his guru's exhilarating recital, set to the harmony of a finely-tuned

tanpura. It was the melody of a *parati* rendered in
bhairavi—the morning song, sung in the morning raga.

> 'O you poor people of Kashi, such trusting folks,
> Ensnared by love, buoyed to scaffolds
> So sings the bird, that lives in Braj.'

O' you poor Mahendar! Hereafter, caged in that soul of
yours, the bird from Braj will chirp forever. Son, you have
buoyed yourself to the scaffold.

The maestro kept on singing, one song after another.
Drenched in that torrent of rasas, his disciples sat motionless,
as if in a state of trance. That morning, a sudden flash of
a divine revelation came to Mahendar. He felt as if he had
witness an otherworldly reality: a timeless truth. Earlier,
whenever his guru had tried introducing him to the soul
of music, he had unwittingly resisted his own initiation
into that mystic world of poetry and melody. But today,
the mysteriously elusive soul of music suddenly revealed
itself to him: layer after layer, all by itself. The last song
of the maestro's morning practice ended, but immersed
in that surreal awakening, Mahendar stood unmindful of
the conclusion.

'Who stands there?' Master's loud gravelly voice
shattered Mahendar's stupor. Overcome with emotions,
he ran to him, clamped his feet and prostrated himself
in reverence. Ramnarayan Misir could feel the warm
tear droplets falling on his feet. Worried at his disciple's

meltdown, he inquired anxiously, 'What is all this, Mahendar? Is everything all right at home? Where are you coming from, son? What is the matter, dear boy?'

But Mahendar kept sobbing inconsolably. A little later, perhaps feeling somewhat unburdened after he had wept to his heart's content, he replied, 'Guru-ji, all these years you wearied yourselves trying to teach me music and help me grasp its essence. But I was so stubborn that I never learnt a thing. But today, after listening to your songs, for the first time in my life, I feel as if a lamp has been lit to dispel all that was dark in me. And in my heart, I can verily see its glow. I feel as if I have crossed over from the dominion of darkness to the sphere of light.' Ramnarayan clutched Mahendar's hands and looked at him fixedly. There was nothing left for him to say.

* * *

The evening congregation was in progress. Ramnarayan turned to Mahendar and said, 'Mahendar, let us start today's session with your recital.'

Mahendar picked up a tanpura and started singing; the first song led to a second, and the second was followed quickly by a third, but Ramnarayan didn't quite like any of them.

'Why do you appear so withdrawn, Mahendar? Are you feeling unwell?' Ramnarayan asked.

'Why, no, Guru-ji, I do feel alright,' Mahendar replied nervously.

'Then sing with gusto, my boy,' said Ramnarayan and let out a gay laughter.

Mahendar was struggling to beat his own hesitation. However, the moment he started singing Dhelabai's song, which has been stirring in his heart ever since the previous night, he somehow hit the right notes too.

'O' beloved, forfeit not my reminiscences.'

The song felt curiously familiar to Ramnarayan. As it progressed, its lyrics reverberated through his soul. He had a dreamlike sensation; clung to its melody, he had retreated into a past that was distant, yet surprisingly vivid. The song ended and the session came to a close. But Ramnarayan did not move. He remained seated, lost in a deep reverie. Mahendar's song had taken him thirty years back into his own past. Back then, he must have been no more than twenty-five or twenty-six. At that young age, for the very first time in his life, he had felt the irresistible enchantment of music. He had come to conclude that of all things alluring in the world, only music could move his soul. Since he had no interest in household chores, and was bored at home, he had started working as an opium inspector with the hallowed Opium Bungalow of Revelgunj. And whenever he had a little time to spare, he was quick to pick up his tanpura. Every time he sang, his resonant voice would splash all around the place, like the waves of the flourishing Saryu. Revelgunj wasn't too far away from Chhapra. Every now and then, he would sneak away to the city to train under Ustaad Najju Khan Sahib. Khan was a descendant of a prominent music family from Lucknow and had shifted permanently to Chhapra. Back in those days, Ramnarayan was brimming over with youthful vigor. His audacious heart, full of raw courage, had emboldened him to strive tirelessly and make a name for himself.

It was at the Opium Bungalow that he had first met Sahay, and almost immediately, formed a close friendship with him. In him, Ramnarayan had found his perfect match. The two were similar in more ways than one. To begin with, they had similar physiques. Like Ramnarayan, Sahay too, was a man with an enormous capacity for perseverance and daring. He too, loved music, although he wasn't obsessively passionate about it. Together, they embarked on many an adventure, seeking pleasure and rasa. Was there any place worth a visit in the entire province those two hadn't travelled to? Was there a song they hadn't heard? Or a dancer whose mujra they hadn't attended? However, in spite of all their indulgent exploits, Sahay did not surrender himself completely to a life of intemperance. Like the leaves of the lotus plant, he had the ability to stay afloat even as he traversed the deep muddy waters of tireless pleasure-seeking. Ramnarayan, by contrast, lost everything to his unbridled obsession with music and mujra. He lost his job at the Opium Bungalow, and like a determined rasik, led the life of an itinerant for years, enjoying mujras

and music wherever he could. But when that feverish
fixation simmered down, he found himself seeking shelter
in Pakadi, his ancestral village. Meanwhile, Haliwant Sahay
had ascended to the summit of his fortune.

* * *

Meenabai of Muzaffarpur had come to Revelgunj. She
had been called to entertain the baraat at the wedding
of Kishan Sahu's daughter. The residents of the Opium
Bungalow were held in high esteem throughout the
mofussil and their attendance was solicited at every social
gathering. As expected, both Sahay and Ramnarayan were
invited to Meenabai's *mehfil*. When Ramnarayan saw
Meenabai, he was hopelessly ensnared by her bewitching
beauty. The luscious fulsomeness of her twenty-year-old
body was brimming over with a seductive allure. Like the
flooded Saryu, her intoxicating charm appeared illimitable
and wild. When she danced, her delicately embroidered
skirt rose and fell, like the waves of the Saryu during *sawan*,
the season of incessant rain and unbounded longing. And
whenever she swirled, her skirt spiralled like a whirlpool in
a river.

'O' beloved, forfeit not my reminiscences.'

That evening, Meenabai sang her sensational love
ballad. Such was the enchantment of her song that
Ramnarayan surrendered his entire being to its melody.
Even though he was completely spellbound and oblivious

to his surroundings, yet he gathered an experience which he could never forget: it was vivid, luminous, colorful and surreal.

In spite of Sahay's repeated attempts to awaken him out of that daydream and get him to leave the party, Ramnarayan remained resolutely unmoved. It was only after the *mehfil* came to a close, and the long sequence of songs ended, that he returned to his senses. As he ambled back to the bungalow, he was amazed to find Sahay engrossed in account-keeping. 'This Kayasth has no appreciation for beauty, no heart,' Ramnarayan thought to himself. When Sahay saw him, he laughed aloud and remarked, 'Dear divine Brahman, if you persist with your reckless ways, you will soon find yourselves a pauper, in the esteemed company of Sudama, Krishna's destitute friend.'

Incensed at the suggestion, Ramnarayan left his job at the Opium Bungalow and embraced a life of vagrancy. Although he drifted about in every direction, he never visited Muzaffarpur; his Brahmanical pride prevented him from seeking after Meenabai. Finally, when that feverish obsession abated, he sought refuge at Pakadi, his own village. What followed was a long period of extreme hardship.

Late in the nights, whenever his cousin's wife toiled at the millstone, she let out a mournful *jantsar*, the grinder's song. The haunting sadness of her complaints ached Ramnarayan's heart. Years ago, in search of employment, his cousin had left for Morang. But he never returned to his wife. The tireless clatter of the whirring millstones and the woebegone tunes of jantsar that streamed forth night after night from the adjacent courtyard, pierced Ramnarayan's heart and made it difficult for him to sleep in the hallway of his dilapidated ancestral house.

The pangs of separation, that he had both witnessed and suffered, metamorphosed into lyrics of poorvi songs. As years went by, he could no longer recall the lines of that famous song which Meenabai had sung at the wedding in Revelgunj. In fact, he had no recollection of Meenabai— the source of an agony which had both ennobled and ruined his life. Over the years, as he scraped a survival in Pakadi, the plaintive tunes of his sister in law's jantsar drowned his personal sorrows.

* * *

But today, thirty years later, that old wound was sore again. The words of that old forgotten song had resurfaced and he could feel its sweltering ardor; it threatened to smolder whatever was of left of him down to a cinder. For a while, Ramnarayan remained speechless. He could see that his disciple was going through the same emotional tumult that he had himself suffered years ago. But how had Mahendar come to learn this song?

'Who taught you that ballad, Mahendar?' Ramnarayan asked.

'Gulzaribai—Meenabai's daughter, It is her song,'

Ramnarayan drew a deep breath. That name carried his thoughts away to the days of his own youth. Back then, when he had sung Meenabai's song, his own guru, Ustaad Najju Khan, had asked him the same question—the very same that he had asked Mahendar.

'Ramnarayan, where did you learn this song?'

'It is Meenabai's song, master.'

Khan did not utter a word of praise, nor did he rebuke Ramnarayan; instead, he subjected his disciple to an unnerving cold stare. When Sahay learnt of the episode, he enjoyed a hearty laugh at the expense of his lovelorn friend.

'Ramnarayan, men do not groan and sigh in vain. They rely on their prowess and seize the things they take a shine to.'

'Haliwant, I have done the same. Seized the things I love: agony, suffering and the unforgettable experience of that evening, everything.'

He remembered how Sahay had burst into a thunderous guffaw at that declaration.

6

The Pet and the Patron

Bulakna Dom had come to live in the village of Bagoeyan with his entire army of clansmen and aides. Across the bamboo orchard, a little further from Bagoeyan's settlement area, a campsite was chosen, and poles and pegs were driven into the ground. In no time the makeshift tents evolved into dozens of shacks and mud houses. Gradually, the Magahiya Doms acquired a little arable tract. Whatever little they owned, the plot of land included, was earned through rewards and grants. Just as pet cheetahs and hawks are rewarded by their owners when they seize a prey, the Doms got these endowments for the services they had rendered: a morsel of desiccated flesh for every fresh and meaty quarry they fetched. Content with that crumb, the Doms never thought much of themselves, or of their toil.

Generations ago, at a time unknown, this group of Magahiya Doms had come to live in Danapur, on the other side of the river Ganga—revered across the region as the Ganga-ji. Later, when the sepoy outposts were being established in the town, the Company administration decided to uproot their entire colony. Thereafter, for a very long time, they simply buzzed around those military camps. Letting go of the land they had lived on for generations was a deeply traumatic experience. Every now and then, whenever they sniffed an opportunity, they would promptly set up tents in the adjoining areas. However, there was nothing certain about those crude dwellings—neither their longevity, nor their location. Life was harsh. At times, sheltered under some tree, they were forced to brave the marrow-piercing cold waves of *Maagh* and *Pausa*—the bitter chill that sweeps the region from December to February.

The confluence of the Ganga-ji and the river Son provided for several necessities of life. During the floods, whenever they had the good fortune to retrieve chattels drifting amidst the deluge, they experienced consummate contentment. Sometimes, they collected honey from combs that sagged under shady canopies of trees; at other times, they chopped down entire trees to sell their timber. However, neither the honey-collection nor the occasional timber-trade was enough to make ends meet. Understandably, survival took more than such irregular activities. Throughout this far-flung territory, the Doms were known to carry out brazen thefts and robberies. And when they conducted those dreaded raids, each one of them participated with the same intrepid zeal—men and women alike.

A few among them had found employment as cleaners and scavengers in the sepoy camps. However, their earnings weren't sufficient to fill their stomachs. Naturally, to supplement their meagre incomes, the men would be on the lookout for the remotest opportunity for stealing, while the women took to seducing the young recruits and extorting money. As expected, every now and then, a ruckus would erupt in that colony of Doms. But no sooner had people drowned themselves in a pour of toddy than all was forgiven and forgotten. By the next dawn, the community sprung back to its old and wonted ways of living.

The Magahiya Doms were blessed with imposing built, shapely physiques and matchless nonchalance. It was for these reasons that Sahay had developed a great fondness for the tribe. When he had seen them for the first time, he was completely awestruck. On the other side of the Saryu, along Chhapra's sizeable river delta, a tent had been put up. With a clean loincloth swathed about his waist, and brandishing a bamboo log with a sharpened end, or maybe a spear, Bulakna had set out on a wild boar hunt. Having tired the boar out after a long pursuit, he impaled its breast with his weapon. The fatally wounded beast dragged itself for some distance, then it dropped dead right in front on Sahay. When Bulakna arrived at the spot to claim the carcass, exhausted and soaked in sweat, each muscle of his shredded body aroused Sahay's awed admiration.

Sahay wasted no time in spinning schemes to trap the Doms into his service. He had read somewhere of the practice of taming cheetahs for hunting purposes; once tamed, even the ferocious animal of prey hunts meekly for its master. Sahay wanted to lure the Doms into becoming his pet cheetahs. Using promise of riches and employment in his opium trade as baits, he whetted their avarice. The itinerant Magahiya Doms, forever adrift like a river current, found a foothold in his promises. Rootless since many monsoons, this group of Doms, after years of bewildered wandering, had arrived at this place for good.

* * *

During the Rebellion of 1857, when the rebel sepoys of Danapur outpost crossed the Son and started marching towards Arrah, the Doms followed them too. It was downright dangerous to stick around an abandoned camp. Since the Doms were accustomed to live off theft and robbery, conducting surprise raids at distant locations had become their forte. Once they reached Arrah along with the sepoys, they joined Babu Kunwar Singh's army and got deputed as messengers and locators. The indomitable Doms were relentless in completing tasks assigned to them. Stormy weather, dense darkness or impassable terrain, they remained undaunted by all hostile circumstances; they could run barefoot through fields covered with prickly stubble; they could slither through slippery riverbanks. Rivers, canals, thorns or sharp-edged wild grass, nothing could stop them.

Marching beside Babu Kunwar Singh, they scouted all the way till Banaras. However, after Kunwar Singh's death, when the English succeeded in suppressing the uprising and a reign of merciless persecution was unleashed, they dispersed. Committing random thefts and robberies, and making merry whenever they could, they entered Balia through Gazipur, before finally setting up a camp along the bank of the Saryu. And then, blinded by the promise of riches, they came under Mukhtar Haliwant Sahay's aegis. Very soon, the wild cheetahs found themselves completely domesticated.

It was this same group of Doms which, obeying Sahay's orders, had invaded the inn in Chhapra and adducted Dhelabai—Meenabai's darling daughter. That breathtakingly beautiful girl, whom Meenabai considered dearer than her own life, was scooped away from the midst of a packed jamboree. To get to Dhelabai, Sahay had tempted the Doms with another lump of flesh: a plot of arable land in Bagoeyan village.

Dawood Khan, the kotwal of the Manjhi police station, remained perennially annoyed by the fact that each night, he had to patrol all the way to Bagoeyan to check on the Doms. Could one think of another drill to restrain this criminal tribe? For the safety of the people in adjoining villages, it was necessary to inspect and count them every single night.

Dawood Khan had once cautioned Sahay against patronising them, 'Mukhtar Sahib, these Magahiya Doms are like mercury, that vilely enigmatic substance. In a split second, they can disperse and disappear, and with the same speed, they can regroup into a scary unit. When mercury enters our body, it resurfaces as leprosy and boils. Could one ever be certain that these Doms would not make lepers out of us?'

Sahay had brushed the warning aside saying, 'Kotwal Sahib, medics produce medicines from mercury and use it to cure several dreaded diseases. My intentions are no different. I wish to transform this treacherous substance into life-giving ambrosia. Please help me with this task.'

When that piece of land was being transferred to the Magahiya Doms, Prasad had laughed and said, 'Mukhtar Sahib, what good is land to them? Will they ever take to farming? They will sell it off and drink away all the proceeds. And after that, like a wandering whirlwind, they will drift to a new place.'

Once again, Babu Haliwant Sahay greeted that suggestion with his irreverent laughter and arrogantly held his view, 'Registrar Sahib, I am the Mukhtar, am I not? All this land will remain registered with this *Kaiser-e-Hind*—this sovereign of a man. What is there for them to sell? They will remain merely chained to the land. Please, let us get on with the registration.'

Indeed, that piece of land was like a rotten lump of flesh. It had succeeded in blinding the cheetahs. The Doms had risked their lives to abduct the gold-like Dhelabai. After delivering her safely to Haliwant Sahay, they were too ecstatic over their new possession and remained utterly contented.

7

An Unexpected Guest

Ever since Dhelabai's arrival at the Red Mansion, extravagant soirées had become an everyday affair. Typically, these soirees commenced late in the evening and went on till early dawn. The finest of artists and the most famous of tawaifs performed at these carnivals of dance and music. All through the night, tablas clopped, sarangis rasped, matchless vocal acrobatics were executed, and the resonant anklet bells tinkled on the Iranian carpet, *chhoom-chhanan*. Cups of wine clunked and fell silent; the seductive effervescence of these parties tested the sobriety of Sahay's friends and the reverentially invited local patricians—affluent zamindars, high-ranking officers and prominent judges. At dawn, when the revellers dispersed, remnants of the night-long gala would lie strewn all over the carpet; shrivelled wreathes of jasmine, haphazardly thrown around bolsters, wheeling empty bottles and broken cups bore witness to the profligacy of the merrymaking. Sometimes, standing quietly by the door that connected the nautch-house to the rest of the mansion, Gulzaribai would look through the drapery and brood over the sight of debauchery.

* * *

But soon Gulzaribai would stop taking part in the everyday gatherings. She would only perform at the private mehfils of Babu Haliwant Sahay—those specially arranged soirées to which no guest was ever invited. On such occasions, she sang the most soulful of melodies and performed astonishing dance recitals, each more spectacular than the previous one. The spectacle unfolded with abundant civility and decorum—no clanking cups, no clanging bottles. Sahay was known to savour the finest of English wines. However, during those jealously guarded evenings, he would not permit even a drop of alcohol to slink down his throat.

Dhelabai could never come to grips with the thought behind this intriguing etiquette. 'Tell me Sahib, why is it that the man whose house overflows with wine remains thirsty himself?' she once asked. Interrogated thus, Haliwant Sahay had merely gawked at her. He did not offer an answer. Even in the company of revellers who guzzled wine, Haliwant Sahay had begun to only sip fruit juice.

But how was Dhelabai to know this secret?

Only Pataluwa, his pet servitor, was aware of this clandestine code of consumption. But Pataluwa himself was astonished to notice how, after the arrival of Dhelabai, his Sahib's extravagant lifestyle had become visibly modest.

* * *

Pataluwa recalled how, within a few weeks of Dhelabai's arrival, Pandit Ramnarayan Misir had come to the Red Mansion, taking everyone by surprise. It was nearing midnight and Dhelabai's mujra was in full swing. Like always, the assembly of merrymakers boasted of powerful officers, the most prominent of judges and the wealthiest of zamindars. The frenzy of dance acts and songs was accompanied by bouts of frantic drinking; bottle after bottle of wine were opened and emptied. In the midst of that wild party, Ramnarayan's sudden appearance had astonished everyone.

That evening, the residents of the Red Mansion saw Ramnarayan for the first time in fifteen years. Pataluwa couldn't even recognize him; his charcoal-black moustache of the yesteryears had greyed like the bark of the Indian hemp; in place of the silk kurta, which always shone on his body, he had put on an austere *mirzaee*—a monk's coarse and rugged garb; in place of his well-groomed hair—long, thick and lubricated generously with perfumed oil—a cropped grey stubble had appeared. Pataluwa mistook him for an average client and addressed him insultingly from a distance, 'O Babu Sahib, where do you think you have come to? This is not your place to be. Go to the White Mansion, the one across the road. You may spend the night in the hallway. It is reserved for clients like you. Hopefully, by tomorrow morning, you may get an opportunity to meet Mukhtar Sahib.'

With his finger pressed against his lip, Gulab Singh, the gatekeeper, entreated Pataluwa to stop. Initially, that gesture made no sense to him. However, under that faint glimmer of the torchlight, when Pataluwa examined the figure closely, he was mortified and fell prostrate at Ramnarayan's feet pleading, 'Baba, I have made a terrible mistake, please pardon me. It was dark and I could not recognise you. Please proceed to the nautch-house, please do.'

Enthralled by the song that came filtering through the closed door, Ramnarayan settled on the reclining chair that was laid out on the veranda. 'No, Pataluwa. I'll sit here and enjoy the soirée. Who is the singer? Could it be Dhelabai? Don't worry about me; go and attend to your chores.'

Pataluwa dashed inside. Song, dance and wine—a cripplingly inebriated Sahay had completely lost himself to that tantalizing ambience. Pataluwa knelt behind him and gently whispered in his ears, 'Sahib, Misir Baba has come.' But Sahay could not gather a word; the clamour of the clinking cups drowned Pataluwa's whispers. He repeated his message once more, but to no avail. Thenceforth, he could not muster enough nerves to make another sound; for someone so adept at deciphering the subtlest of instructions and keeping his master pleased, he knew full well what his boundaries were. For the rest of the evening, he scurried in and out of the nautch-house—fetching bottles of wine from the camphorwood cupboard, carrying elegantly served kebabs from the kitchen, and kneading Ramnarayan's fatigued legs, or fanning him, whenever he got a little respite from the soirée.

Just then, the inn's tower-clock struck one and its bell gonged, *tann*. Dhelabai was startled by the sound. Her anklet bells went out of tune and the beats broke off. The drunken revellers saw her run away into the inner wings of the mansion. Dhelabai's abrupt departure put a quietus on the revelries. The soiree stood dissolved and everyone started tottering out. Buggy after buggy came and ferried away the wobbly revellers. Some went alone, others went in pairs. Clattering along the gravelled red lane, the carriages drove out of the gate. *Tik, tik!* Like a perfect host, Sahay stood by the porch to bid his guests goodbye. Each time a carriage was ready to depart, he warmly shook the hands of its occupant. This was also a signal for the occupants of the next carriage to descend the steps. As the last guest left, Pataluwa approached him and gently announced again, 'Sahib, Misir-ji has come.'

'Where is he?' asked Sahay, thrilled to bits. By then Ramnarayan had left his chair and climbed down the steps to meet his friend. They ran towards one another and united in a warm embrace. Pataluwa's Sahib was a 'real' sahib indeed; whoever he met or spoke to, his proud and distinguished bearing called attention to his lofty status. Like a true sahib, he always soared in the sky, distant from the earthbound mortals. With his mere gaze, he could set things aflame and unnerve people, as the sahibs were known to do. And yet, upon seeing Ramnarayan, look how he sloughed that snakeskin of his! With his friend around him, he had started behaving like an overjoyed little boy. Admittedly, Pataluwa was somewhat worried at the transformation.

At last, Sahay's carriage drove up to the porch, but he ignored it with a lordly abandon and started walking towards the White Mansion, holding Ramnarayan's hands. When Bulakna picked up his spear and tried to escort the duo, Sahay forbade him from following him. Pataluwa had no choice but to run ahead of them to the mansion and make arrangements for the unexpected guest.

* * *

Ramnarayan's reunion with Sahay took fifteen long years. All those years ago, following a heated spat, he had thrown his shawl across his shoulder and walked out of the White Mansion—on foot, without waiting for a carriage or a palanquin. Pataluwa had vivid memories of that inauspicious day. He recalled how Sahay kept pacing up and down the veranda, his fists clinched in agitation.

And then, as his restlessness became unbearable, he darted towards the gate. For a very long time, he stood quietly at the mansion's entrance, staring in keen anticipation at the road that ran through the Bhagwan Bazaar. But his wait was long and disappointing. Disheartened, he retreated slowly to his room, stretched himself on his bed and pulled a sheet over his face. Months passed and then years, but since that day, Ramnarayan had never stepped into the mansion; the man known to stop by every fortnight, and spend a few days on each visit, had not shown up even once in all these years. Pataluwa couldn't guess the reason. Back then, he was just a little boy who held Sahay in mortal fear. He could never bring himself to ask his master anything about Ramnarayan. But he had eavesdropped on others talking about the matter, and heard a few murmurs about marriage and such things. These he still remembered.

The room where Ramnarayan stayed during his visits was adjacent to Sahay's own bedroom. Back in those days, it was known as Misir Baba's room, and it still bore his name. However, ever since his acrimonious disappearance, it had remained bolted. Having run to the White Mansion ahead of the two, Pataluwa opened that room and started dusting it. Meanwhile, accompanied by Ramnarayan, Sahay arrived too. Addressing Pataluwa in his roaring voice, he instructed from a distance, 'O Pataluwa, Misir-ji's bed will be set in my room.'

It was late at night and the entire mansion was fast asleep. Pataluwa slept on the veranda. Every now and then, weary of lugging the strings of the *pankha*—the swinging cloth-fan suspended across the ceiling—Bhageluwa dozed off too. But the two friends, estranged for ages, kept gossiping all night long.

It must have been early dawn, about four by the clock; Orion was beginning to fade away from the horizon and the brilliant Venus had presently ascended. Roused by the clatter, Pataluwa opened his bleary eyes and saw both Sahay and Ramnarayan get into a carriage. Soon, the vehicle sped away and Bulakna sprinted behind it, clutching his formidable spear. Later that day, he learnt from Bulakna that they had gone to Revel Sahib's grave along the bank of the Saryu. He also got to know that Sahay had knelt by the grave and spent nearly two hours in quiet contemplation. Later, the two visited the old Opium Mansion to relive their olden days. After a quick breakfast, they set out for their respective destinations: Ramnarayan left on foot for Pakadi, while Sahay returned to Chhapra, riding his carriage.

8

A Secret Pact

Pataluwa was completely baffled; for the past ten days or so, Sahay had confined himself to his room. If ever a visitor came, he would merely send out a message feigning illness. In the meantime, he had stopped drinking altogether. Not a single drop of wine had trickled down his throat. During the evenings, when Prasad came over to pay his customary visit, he would have him summoned straight to his bedroom. Prasad was always greeted with a cup of wine, which, sitting in Sahay's unusually quiet company, he sipped at slowly. 'I am in poor health' or 'the doctor has forbidden me to drink': with these stock excuses, he managed to dodge alcohol every time.

This humdrum went on for nearly fifteen or twenty days. Meanwhile, Vidyadharibai had arrived from Banaras.

She enjoyed a towering reputation. When she came to the
Red Mansion, she was given a rousing reception. Even Sahay
sprung back to his feet to welcome her. Arrangements for
her mehfil soon got underway. Messengers were dispatched
in every direction to deliver invites. Around evening,
Pataluwa saw Ramnarayan walk in through the gate. He
was accompanied by a young man. Without wasting a
moment, Pataluwa ran inside to inform his Sahib of their
arrival. However, he could not relay his message as he was
completely astounded by the sight he had stumbled upon;
the shrine room had been unlocked after ages, and inside
the room, Sahay was down on his knees, staring absorbedly
at Revel Sahib's portrait. Pataluwa did not have the courage
to interrupt his Sahib's meditation. He merely stood at the
door, unmoving and shocked. After a long time, Sahay
opened his eyes and rose to his feet. Pataluwa could see a trail
of tears that had streamed down his eyes and drenched his
cheeks. He thought of edging away from the door, mortified
at the sight, but Sahay saw him and called out, 'Pataluwa, is
that you?'

Sahay was equally embarrassed and didn't know what
to say. After a brief pause, he overcame his indecision and
spoke gravely in a tone of authority, 'Pataluwa, this day
onwards, I entrust you with a great responsibility. I want
you to know that I have completely renounced alcohol. This
is the vow I took at Revel Sahib's grave. But none should
ever know of it. As earlier, cups of alcohol will be handed
around at my parties, but the one served to me will hold
nothing except fruit juice. And all this must be carried out

in absolute secrecy. Is that understood? No one is to discover that my cup holds juice, not wine. Do you understand?'

'Yes, Sahib,' Pataluwa replied meekly.

That same evening, the Red Mansion hosted Vidyadharibai's mujra. The nautch-house was packed with zamindars, judges, officers and artists. Vidyadhari or the bearer of art. She was one of the foremost exponents of the art of singing. Her mastery over the nuances of music was esteemed and acknowledged throughout India. As expected, she did not disappoint her patrons.

Mahendar was also present in the mehfil. Awed by the tall statures of men who had swarmed the nautch-house, he sat shrivelled in a corner. Everyone waited eagerly for Gulzaribai to make an appearance in Vidyadharibai's mujra. Wasn't it only fifteen or twenty days ago that they had assembled for her performance? But today, their yearnings for the flame that had brightened many a mehfil remained unfulfilled. To the disappointment of everyone, Gulzaribai sat quietly behind the drapes all through the evening.

At the very outset, Vidyadharibai touched Pandit Ramnarayan Misir's feet, sought his blessings and launched a spirited rendition of a thumri.

'O' beloved,
Pray, do not hurl marigolds thus,
It hurts my heart.'

With each sentiment that she stirred, every note that she hit, and all those subtle intonations that she so deftly executed, her spellbound connoisseurs grew more and more restless with ecstasy; like a helpless snake slithering on an oiled floor, they struggled to get a grip over their senses. The first song was followed by another thumri, then a composition in the *dadar,* and finally, a *tappa.* Enchanted by her recitals, the spectators were transported to another realm of existence—a make-believe pleasure land.

At this point, Ramnarayan intervened and said, 'Vidyadhari, you are the empress of this mehfil. Your music is beyond description, like the invigorating touch of a serene breeze. But today, I want you to listen to this boy here—my disciple—whom I have brought along to your mehfil. Let him sing once too.'

Approaching Ramnarayan, Vidyadharibai bowed, touched his feet again and smilingly replied, 'Master, your wish is a sacred command. But no one dares to sing after Vidyadhari's performance.'

Ramnarayan laughed and added, 'Indeed, Vidyadhari. You are right. But this boy is a naive rustic. I am sure he wouldn't be so diffident as not to sing after you. Give him a chance.' At Ramnarayan's command, Mahendar picked up the tanpura, touched the master's feet and started singing.

'O' precious son,
I would have returned home,
Earlier than early morning,
Had I known dear Ram would come,
To our humble dwelling.'

The haunting melody of that poorvi enthralled the entire gathering. Tears poured out of Sahay's eyes too. Vidyadharibai was stunned into silence. Even Gulzaribai could not contain her excitement. The drapes of the Red Mansion were partially lifted and twinkling like a firefly, a pair of refulgent eyes beheld the spectacle elatedly.

* * *

As soon as Mahendar finished his song, Vidyadharibai sought Ramnarayan's leave and disappeared hastily into the inner wing of the mansion. The mehfil came to a close and people started clearing out of the nautch-house. Mahendar was the last one to leave. But barely had he reached the exit when Pataluwa intercepted him and asked him to stop. He obliged him and turned back. The sight that greeted his eyes had him both riveted and puzzled: in front of him stood Gulzaribai, her eyes wet with tears. Unsure of how to strike a conversation, the young man with bewildered instincts started digging the earthen floor with his toenail. Gulzaribai thrust a tiny packet in his hand and said softly, 'Misir-ji, to me, your song was like a shower of divine bliss. Although it is not my place to reward you, I beg you to accept this modest gift. Pray, treasure it forever.'

And then, she walked away leisurely, past the drapes, into the mansion. Clutching the packet, Mahendar stepped out of the nautch-house, his body completely soaked in sweat. He hurried across the street, reached the White Mansion and settled on a bed that was kept in the guest room. For quite a while, he just held on to that packet; perhaps too diffident to open it and find out what it concealed within. Finally, having regained his confidence somewhat, he brought himself to unwrap it.

'Good Lord! What is this? Gulzaribai's nose ring!'

9

She Is No Harlot

Sahay looked thoroughly exhausted upon his return from Pakadi; his face was scorched, his tired eyes red. His silken angrakha, covered with sweat and dust, had become clammy. No sooner had he arrived than he climbed into his bed and slept for hours, like a lifeless log. By the time he woke up, Pataluwa had already placed buckets of water in the washroom. Having washed and changed, he felt a little revived. Soon, dinner was served by Yusuf Miyan, the mansion's loyal old cook. Sahay ambled to the dining room, but returned without eating anything. 'Pataluwa, I will have only curd today,' he announced.

Pataluwa always shadowed his Sahib with unquestioning obedience. That evening, too, he kept staring blankly at his Sahib's face and waited for instructions. As soon as the command was issued, he ran to the kitchen and returned quickly with a bowl of curd in hand. A little later, the cook was sent for; Yusuf was prompt in answering the call. With his head bowed and palms joined in a namaskar, he stood in a gesture of deep obeisance.

'Yusuf Miyan, you have grown old. You spent your entire life serving Revel Sahib and me, yet neither he nor I have done anything for you.' Sahay took a long pause after the candid admission. Meanwhile, an astounded Yusuf waited in nervous silence, unsure of what lay in store for him.

'Listen, it is my wish that after all these years of dreary toil, you must now rest. And spend your days in contemplation of God. Man needs time for prayers, too, doesn't he? If there is any pursuit of yours that remains incomplete, you should tell me. I'll see to its completion.'

Having made that promise, he grew quiet again and turned his eyes skywards, as if trying to seek something out in that starlit expanse. Wasn't it only yesterday that Ramnarayan, his friend for life, had departed for his heavenly abode? He was mortified by the realization that just as he had failed Yusuf Miyan, he had failed his friend too; neither could he honour any of his wishes, nor could he support any of his endeavours. There wasn't the faintest trace of selfishness in what Ramnarayan desired. His wishes were always linked to Sahay's happiness, prosperity and good reputation. But blinded by the obstinacy of youth and crazed by the power of money, he could never understand Ramnarayan's selfless friendship. And what's more, he had wounded him with his bitter words and expelled him from his mansion.

For fifteen long years, the two soulmates had seared in a strange fire; it was neither fanned by spite, nor by repentance. Indeed, the years of separation had caused an intense agony to both. Yet, five years ago, when Sahay had Dhelabai abducted, Ramnarayan had buried all his long-harboured grudges and rushed to give his friend a sage counsel. Finding him alone, Ramnarayan had said, 'Dear Haliwant, is this not what I always wanted for you: a woman to look after you and your household? But you fought with me whenever I made that suggestion. Well, what's done cannot be undone. Henceforth, please let good sense prevail upon you. Do not trifle with the honour of the woman whom you have welcomed into your household.'

Like always, Babu Haliwant Sahay laughed at the advice dispensed to him and asked, 'Brother Misir, do you reckon that she is my lawfully wedded wife?'

Ramnarayan, too, had a hearty laugh at his friend's counter-question, but he tried to reason with him saying, 'So, is she the harlot from Muzaffarpur? Brother, let me tell you this: the harlot has long perished—dead, since that night in the inn. This one here, who lives in your mansion, whether married or a mere concubine, is Babu Haliwant Sahay's woman.'

That day onwards, Dhelabai never stepped out of purdah to perform in public.

* * *

Yusuf Miyan slumped lifelessly at Sahay's feet, clasped his legs and wept, 'Sahib, please do not drive me out. It will be the end of the road for me. I have no one but you to call my own. My wife is dead, so is my son. Where would I find refuge at this age? I beg you; please do not throw me out.'

Sahay was presently lost in memories of the days gone by, but Yusuf Miyan's heart-rending entreaties pulled him back to the present. 'Oh! Yusuf Miyan! Why do you weep? Could I ever throw you out? You were recruited by Revel Sahib. Would I ever have the moral courage to fire you? Look, all I am saying is now that you have become very old, you need some time to yourself; a little time to be spent remembering Allah!'

As he uttered these words to assuage Yusuf, a sobering thought came into his mind: 'Is there anyone other than Yusuf Miyan whom I can call my own?' Exhaling deeply, Sahay continued, 'Yusuf Miyan, you see, Misir bhai is no more. Last evening, he gave up this earthly mirzaee—the one we jealously guard and call our body. During those final moments, he just held on to my hand. Although not a world could pass through his lips, but it felt as if he had said everything; all that was there to be told. Now, I can sense that time is running out for me too. I should also turn my thoughts to Ram.'

Comforted by these words of assurance, Yusuf released his hold on Sahay's legs, rose to his feet and wiped his tears. Looking sorrowful and dejected by the unexpected turn of events, he trudged away, stoically mumbling to himself, 'Master, now I get it. I get it all. Misir Baba never touched the food I cooked. But he would always tell me: Yusuf, make sure your Sahib is well fed. Now I get it, master. So it shall be.' Sahay stood quietly and watched Yusuf Miyan go.

Although Pataluwa was known to turn a blind eye to the affairs of the mansions and always keep mum, yet he could see a pattern in Sahay's behaviour that caused him to worry; Sahay's decision to give up meat had the same impulsiveness about it with which he had given up alcohol some five years ago. Thereafter, his meals were prepared in Tiwari-ji's kitchen, not by Yusuf. Yet, each day, quite unfailingly, Yusuf remembered to unlatch his kitchen's door. After spending a little time in his workshop of many years, he would walk over to Tiwari-ji's kitchen, carefully supervise the meal services, and then retire to his room.

'Pataluwa, see to it that Yusuf Miyan does not suffer any inconvenience. You must bring him meat whenever he craves for it,' said Sahay, certain of his order.

But taking a cue from his master, Yusuf, too, had become a vegetarian. Had he also been overtaken by thoughts of dying, like his master? Yes, it was indeed the autumn of his life. One day, as he knelt to offer namaz, he froze in that posture. After a long anxious wait, when Pataluwa touched him with his nervous hands, his lifeless body rolled down on the floor. On that day, tears had welled up in Sahay's eyes and he did not eat anything.

* * *

For the past few years, Pataluwa had wondered why Sahay's exuberant mehfils were becoming more and more desolate. In the past, these musical galas were graced by the likes of Vidyadharibai, Kesarbai, Janakibai, Roshanaara and many other legendary singers; sometimes they performed at the Red Mansion, on other occasions, the White Mansion hosted them. However, of late, the tawaifs were restricted to the White Mansion. They came to Sahay for old time's sake and left without performing most of the time. If at all a mehfil was organized, it was arranged restrictively at the White Mansion; no one even dared to suggest the Red Mansion as a possible venue.

Before long, the mehfils at the White Mansion became a rarity too. Yet, each day, Gulzaribai would dress up, get into a palanquin and visit Haliwant Babu, as if bound by a sacred duty. During such calls, she was always accompanied by her waiting-woman Jiriya. After spending a little time in Sahay's company, and singing a few of his favourite songs, Gulzaribai would promptly return to the Red Mansion. Prasad was the only other acquaintance who paid regular visits to the White Mansion. He, too, would gossip for a while and then leave. However, loneliness did not seem to bother Sahay anymore; he seemed to have embraced a life of solitude. He spent long hours in the shrine room and stayed wide-eyed till late into the night. Yet, during work hours, he went about his daily business with the same agility and sharpness that he had displayed all his life.

In the past few months, Pataluwa had become somewhat scared of Sahay. He struggled to make sense of the new trends that he saw at the White Manson; there was a steady decline in the frequency of mujras and a clear increase in the number of singers and classical instrumentalists whom Sahay patronised. It wasn't as if the luxuriant soirees of Sahay had stopped altogether, but he had started showing a noticeably greater enthusiasm for bhajans and *nirguns*. The likes of Nassir Khan Beenkar, Bhagwat Maharaj and Lochan Prasad had now become frequent visitors to his place.

Whenever these devotional gatherings were planned, Gulzaribai made sure to come to the White Mansion. And Jiriya used to be her steady escort during each of those excursions. Back then, Jiriya's youth was just about beginning to blossom. Quite understandably, her tender heart, burning with youthful desire, showed no patience for songs of devotion and renunciation. Whenever songs of this variety were sung, she grimaced and quickly disappeared from the venue. But Pataluwa always waited for such songs.

Ramnarayan and his disciple Mahendar had been regular to these gatherings. Mahendar had become a crowd-pleaser; every time he was called upon to present his recitals, he had his audience enthralled. There was one song in particular which created a sensation of sorts.

'O beloved!
As I kneaded your head,
Shoved by your elbow,
My nose ring got mislaid.'

Whenever he sung that song, his enraptured audience swayed and rocked, as if in a state of trance. But Gulzaribai's reaction was rather restrained and peculiar; she would grow oddly quiet, shut her eyes and rest her head against the wall. Both Jiriya and Pataluwa had noticed this strange behaviour.

Sadly, the newly-introduced tradition of devotional gatherings turned out to be a rather short-lived one, coming to an abrupt end the day Ramnarayan passed away. When Sahay got to know that his friend was on his deathbed, he set out immediately for Pakadi. When he returned to Chhapra, he was completely shattered and weighed down by grief. Soon, Sahay's own health started giving way. Worried about Sahay's condition, Gulzaribai devoted herself to nursing him. Owing partly to the restorative power of time, and partly to Gulzaribai's incessant tending, signs of recovery were soon noticeable.

Once he got a little better, he took Gulzaribai along and left for Revel Sahib's bungalow.

Revelgunj was the place he had the fondest memories of; it was here that he had spent the best part of his early years. Its soil restored some of his depleted vigour. For the entire duration of his joyful stay, he paid daily visits to Revel Sahib's grave. He sat by it quietly and meditated for hours. One day, he had a surreal vision; he felt as if Revel Sahib had risen from his grave and was presently addressing him, his arms outstretched. 'Haliwant, this world is huge. Explore its variety; do not stagnate and stink like water trapped in a ditch. You must open up a little.' The vision shattered his quiescence.

He bowed at the grave and gently whispered, 'Father, why did you not come to my rescue earlier? Here I am, at the final stage of my life; what can I possibly do now?'

'Haliwant, words like "then" and "now" are nothing but frothy excuses. Each day is an opportunity to make a new beginning,' the voice answered.

The sensation was so strong that he felt as if Revel Sahib stood close by and spoke to him in his gruff voice. For Sahay, it was a moment of awakening from a deep slumber. That same day, he returned to Chhapra.

* * *

A few days later, Mahendar arrived at the Red Mansion. Traumatized by his guru's death, he looked rather gaunt.

Before dying, Ramnarayan had instructed his disciple to seek refuge at his friend's home. 'Mahendar, should you ever need anything, go to Haliwant,' Ramnarayan had assured. But in spite of that assurance, now that Ramnarayan was gone, Mahendar appeared quite windswept and edgy. It was the first time that he had come to the Red Mansion without being accompanied by his guru. Sahay saw him the moment he got off the carriage. Gulzaribai noticed him too, but she withdrew quickly to the inner wing.

That same day, Mahendar launched his epic narration of Ram's legend in the courtyard of the White Mansion. It was also the first time when the majestic gates of the mansion were thrown open for the commoners. Day after day, he composed delectable songs on episodes from Ramayana and sang them to the delight of his captivated audience. Many a time, those heartfelt compositions moved Sahay to tears. Soon, the narration reached the point where Ram courts Sita in Janakpur's pleasure garden.

'If only I knew,
It was dear Sita's wedding,
To my heart's content,
I would have decorated the nuptial lodging.'

As Mahendar recited these lines, rasa poured on the congregation and the devotees found themselves lost in that otherworldly experience. Suddenly, Sahay had an odd inkling; he felt as if Revel Sahib was calling out to him.

Even though he was surrounded by people on all sides, he decided to get up and catch a glimpse of Revel Sahib's portrait.

When he reached the shrine room, he was surprised to notice that its door was unlatched and the wooden panes were merely huddled together. He pushed them open out of curiosity. His eyes caught sight of two silhouettes that appeared to quiver under the pale light of an earthen lamp. It made him shudder with shock and disgust. 'Goodness! Pataluwa and Jiriya!' he cried out. Retracing his steps hastily, he latched the door and darted to his bedroom. A wad of banknotes lay neglected on a shelf in his bedroom. He grabbed it frenziedly and pulled out the key to his safe from underneath the pillow. As he yanked the safe open, his late wife's ornaments spilled out on the floor: first the *maang teeka* jangled, and then the bracelets clanked, followed by a few necklaces and earrings. He scooped the scattered ornaments up and prepared to leave, his mind still racing. But as he approached the door, his late wife's vermillion case caught his attention; it was shoved in a corner of the safe. That, too, was collected. Using a bedspread, he drew everything together in an untidy bundle and then reached for his gun that dangled high from a hook on the wall. Meanwhile, Mahendar's recital was in full swing. One could hear his resonant voice even from Sahay's bedroom.

He opened the door of the shrine room and found both Pataluwa and Jiriya trembling with fear. Sahay barged

in and yelled, 'Pataluwa, open this vermillion case and put
a red mark across Jiriya's forehead.' Pataluwa froze in fear.
But Sahay had no patience. Aiming his gun at him, he
issued a grim warning, 'Do what I say or . . .'

Pataluwa opened the case and mottled the parting in
Jiriya's hair, as instructed. One could still hear Mahendar
crooning in the background.

'Jiriya, put on the ornaments.'

Jiriya stood unmoving.

'I demand that you wear them immediately.'

Terrified, Jiriya did as he said.

'Pataluwa, with Revel Sahib as your witness, swear that
your will never abandon her.'

Pataluwa knelt down in front of Revel Sahib's portrait.

'Jiriya, now it's your turn. Pledge lifelong fidelity to
Pataluwa.'

Jiriya knelt besides Pataluwa, looking straight at Revel
Sahib's portrait.

Sahay pushed the wad of banknotes into Pataluwa's
trembling hands and said, 'Take Jiriya along and run away
to Sheetlapur. Use this money to buy a farm for yourselves.'

But Pataluwa stood speechless, his head hung in shame.
Annoyed at his silence, Sahay thundered, 'Bastard, run or
I will shoot you dead.'

'Master, how could I leave . . .' Pataluwa whimpered.

Enraged at his obstinacy, Haliwant shouted at him and
said, 'Run. Without wasting a moment, run. Can't you
hear Mahendar Misir's song describing Ram's courtship at

Janakpur? It portends a new beginning for the two of you. Run or this haunted mansion will eat you alive, just as it has eaten me up.'

Pataluwa was filled with a sense of shame and remorse. Without uttering another word, the two bade adieu to the White Mansion. As they were about to leave, Sahay summoned Bulakna and said, 'Bulakna, escort them till the boundary of Sheetlapur. And see to it that it remains a secret.'

10

Parting Lessons

As soon as Mahendar finished his daily recitation of the holy legend of Ram, the search for Jiriya started. 'Jiriya, O Jiriya,' Gulzaribai called out. But those calls remained unanswered. The gathering was dissolved for the day and the devotees had left for their homes. After a frustrating wait, Gulzaribai set out for the Red Mansion, but her waiting-woman wasn't there either. Agitated at her odd disappearance, she ran back to the White Mansion to look again, before retreating shortly in considerable disappointment. Without much delay, Gulzaribai sent for servants of both the mansions and launched a frantic search for Jiriya.

Sahay retired to his room and dozed off, a mysterious smile playing on his face. The night-long search for Jiriya went on until dawn, yet she remained untraceable. Feeling helpless, Gulzaribai came over to Sahay's room and shook him vigorously, 'Are you awake? Please get up. We cannot find Jiriya.'

Sahay opened his languid eyes, yawned and offered his commentary on the ongoing clamour, 'Hmm! Jiriya is untraceable. Is that so? Well, in that case, I'll have to ask you to stop thinking about her, Gulzari. You won't find her ever again. She must have flown away from the mansion, like a fledgling flies away from its nest. Besides, let us not forget that she is, after all, the waiting-woman of a harlot.'

'Shut up!' Gulzaribai shouted, boiling over with anger. 'Don't you feel ashamed? All these years, you had me locked away from people—always behind purdah—yet you have the temerity to call me a harlot! Mark my words, I am not Dhelabai anymore. I am Gulzari Devi. Never ever forget this.'

Sahay was taken aback by her unexpectedly belligerent retort. Hadn't Ramnarayan said the exact same things? However, back then, he had put on such airs that it prevented him from acknowledging what was now glaringly obvious. He could hear the words of Ramnarayan ring into his ears: 'Haliwant, Dhelabai is long since dead. This woman is Gulzari Devi—your woman. Whether lawfully wedded or a mere concubine, she is Haliwant Sahay's woman all the same.'

Five years ago, he had ridiculed that suggestion. But now, it had resurfaced as an undeniable truth. Throughout his life, Sahay had subordinated the expectations of the world, big or modest, to his bloated self-conceit. Reality was always warped to match his convenience. But the truth which Ramnarayan wanted him to honour appeared rather steady and rigid. However, the thought of having a settled way of life with a woman somehow agitated him. Could it be so that the Sahay, who was known to fiercely guard his personal freedom, was getting increasingly tied down to his mansion and to Gulzaribai? No! That must not come to pass! He must protect his freedom and escape the snares of the world, just as his mentor Revel Sahib had. He could not risk staying chained to his desolate mansion, as if it were a valuable possession.

He called to mind the last days of Revel Sahib, the master of the stately Opium Bungalow. When he had come to India, he had brought along the typical English love for pomp and luxuries. However, during his final days, the man had torn himself away from the same opulence which had hitherto defined him. Bequeathing the decrepit edifice of his material possessions to a fool like Sahay, he had cleverly evaded all the entrapments of the world.

For the rest of his years, he surrendered himself to a life of renunciation and lived like a homeless mendicant; he held on to a medicine box and assiduously embraced a saintly life, forfeiting all comforts and excesses. As he went around treating the poor and the sickly, he was the living image of Saint Xavier. He roamed carefree across the province, seeking shelter at random homes whenever it got dark, and asking around for food whenever he felt hungry.

Sahay had pleaded with him to abandon his itinerant life, 'Sahib, please stay with me. It breaks my heart to see you suffer such daily hardship.'

Revel Sahib had dismissed the plea with a laugh and said, 'Haliwant, this is turning out to be the most rewarding phase of my life. Earlier, during those long years that I have lived, I suffered so much. Now, at this ripe age, I have come to realize that every household in the province is like my own home, and these people are like my own children.'

Revel Sahib did not die within the confines of his bungalow; he breathed his last at Gango Padayen's place, under the open sky. When the end drew near, the entire community came together to pay its last respects to him. He departed bidding adieus and bestowing benedictions. Sahay was then in Chhapra. As soon as the news reached him, he rushed to Revelgunj. The funeral procession was quite grand; a huge contingent of mourners trailed the coffin carrying Revel Sahib's body, singing devotional songs to the accompaniment of drums and cymbals. The procession stopped briefly at his bungalow, before heading towards its final destination on the bank of the Saryu. A grave was dug next to the memsahib's. Sahay tried to convince the priest at the Church in Chhapra to preside over the interment, but without success. With slogans like 'Victory to Revel Baba' rending the air, he was laid down at his final resting place. The effusive outpouring of grief and the heartfelt display of devotion had the same intensity with which people bid farewell to saints and seers. Later, a funeral feast was thrown at the bungalow.

When Sahay recalled Revel Sahib's funeral procession, he was also reminded of the last days of Ramnarayan. By the time Sahay had reached Pakadi, Ramnarayan had grown too frail to speak. He called to mind how his old friend had clasped his hands. Holding him thus, a misty-eyed Ramnarayan had merely cast expectant glances at him. Although no words were spoken, yet Sahay felt as though his friend had taught him the most valuable lesson of his life. To drive that lesson home, Ramnarayan had striven so very hard, albeit unsuccessfully. He had tried unremitting persuasion and occasional quarrels; he had seethed during fifteen years of separation; he had buried memories of humiliation, forgiven without an apology, and returned of his own to counsel his friend; he had even sung songs and lectured him tirelessly. Yet, he couldn't make his friend see the worth of that lesson. However, that day, through a simple touch, Sahay could grasp the essence of his friend's words.

* * *

Gulzaribai pleaded through her sobs, 'What useless thoughts are you lost in? Please send your servants to look for Jiriya.'

Sahay sat upright on his bed, smiled and spoke reassuringly, 'Do not worry, Gulzari. I will send Pataluwa right away.' His smile broadened into a grin as he called out loudly, 'Pataluwa!'

But how was Pataluwa to respond to his master's call. '*Arrey*, Pataluwa!' he repeated his summon, feigning surprise and anger. There was no question of a reply. After waiting for a few moments, he turned to Gulzaribai and said playfully, 'You look tired, Gulzari; go and get a little rest. You won't find her again. It appears to me that Pataluwa has run away with your Jiriya, that too from the midst of a gathering.' Gulzaribai cast a stinging sidelong glance at Sahay, wiped her tears off and went away with a smile of relief. Since that day, no one tried looking for either Jiriya or Pataluwa.

But the incident had amplified Sahay's preoccupations manifold. Day after day, he spent long hours updating accounts with his manager Shivdharilal. At times, both were carted off in a carriage to places unknown to Gulzaribai. When evenings came, Sahay picked up his walking-stick and went out to take long solitary strolls. His nights were spent in Gulzaribai's company; she sang a few bhajans and thereafter, the two gossiped till late. Whenever Sahay brought up a matter related to his zamindari, intricate or simple, Gulzaribai would panic and cry out in exasperation, 'Hey Ram! This brings my head to ache.'

'When I was first burdened with these responsibilities, this is exactly how I felt. My head ached too. But once I got a hang of it, I started relishing them,' saying so, Sahay tried to laugh the matter away and change the subject of their conversation. But, before long, they found themselves returning to it, talking about matters concerning property, opium trade and such. Soon, legal documents, too, found their way into these discussions. For Gulzaribai—who was quite cut-off from the tough world of business dealings and estate management—it was all too puzzling. She was often found reiterating her pet grievance: 'I'll never come to grips with this. It makes me hopelessly confused.'

But Sahay merely laughed at her show of irritation and said, 'Gulzari, there is no getting away. Munshi-ji has become very old. We can't expect him to manage everything on his own. And as you know, the law court keeps me very busy.'

But that day, Gulzaribai noticed something that rattled her: the tendrils of grey hair on Sahay's head caused a great upheaval in her heart. She felt as if it was Sahay, and not Shivdharilal, who had aged after all. Suddenly, her vision was clouded by a strange darkness and she felt dizzy. However, she somehow reined in her emotions and put on a smile.

This went on for sometime. In Pataluwa's absence, Gulzaribai took charge of the everyday needs of Sahay. But the responsibility wasn't as strenuous as it used to be. Sahay had limited his personal needs considerably. There was hardly any time for the small indulgences he was known to take delight in; the affairs of the opium trade and the zamindari left him with no time to spare. Keen on relieving Sahay of his burden, Gulzaribai started assisting him with his business dealings; she began shouldering responsibilities of the kind she had dreaded all along. But she could sense that his business was beginning to tail off. And one day, dog-tired after a lifetime of hard work, he left his estate in Shivdharilal's care and got ready to leave for Revelgunj—perhaps setting out on a long-awaited withdrawal from the din of the everyday world. When Gulzaribai offered to go with him, he simply laughed and added, 'Would I get any rest if you are around? The troubles of household chores will continue to hound me.'

None had the pluck to question his decision; as Sahay prepared to relocate to Revelgunj, one could only be a silent bystander. He was determined to live all by himself; no servant or aide was to accompany him. Before boarding the carriage, he bade farewell to each one of his folks. As soon as the vehicle started moving, Bulakna grabbed his spear and started running behind it. Seeing him Sahay smiled affectionately and surrendered to his childlike persistence, 'All right. Come along.' Once the carriage moved past the entrance, it stopped for a moment. Those who had followed it till the gate were staring keenly in its direction. Jutting his head out, Sahay inspected the crowd. He looked around, as if to soak up the memories of the place. And then, his carriage sped off. Bulakna had planted himself firmly on the carriage's foot-stand, spear in his hand.

Later that day, a vacant carriage returned to Chhapra.
Sahay hadn't allowed it beyond the main entrance of the
Opium Mansion. The following day, a teary-eyed Bulakna
returned too and presented himself to Gulzaribai. He
was carrying a bunch of papers. Tormented by ominous
premonitions, Gulzari inquired nervously, 'And what
about Sahib, Bulakna?'

He handed over the papers, including a letter from
Sahay, and stood attentively for further instructions.
His head was bowed and his arms crossed over his chest.
Gulzaribai was on pins and needles. Her hands trembled
in nervous anticipation as she opened the letter. She could
easily recognize the handwriting; it was unmistakably
Haliwant Sahay's. She started reading it, her mind clouded
with trepidations:

Blessed Gulzari,

Haliwant Sahay sends his benedictions. As you know,
Revel Sahib was both a father and a mentor to me.
Having returned to his bungalow, I experience great
tranquillity. When I came here, I discovered Revel
Sahib's old medicine-box; it was lying abandoned on
his table. Due to years of neglect, it was coated with a
thick layer of with dust. I have scoured it clean.

So far, I have seared and suffered all by myself. All
my life, I have endured several tragedies, most of which
was caused by my egoism.

I finally sense that there is a little happiness in store for me too. In his death, Misir Bhai has brightened several roads through which I may escape this dark maze called the world. And when I came here, Revel Sahib's dust-coated medicine box made everything clear as daylight.

During my time, I have fought many battles. But each one of those was actually a struggle against my own self. And even as these battles raged on, at last, I can sense victory.

I have divided my entire property in two halves. One half, along with the Red Mansion, goes to you; the other half, together with the White Mansion, will go to my blood relatives. As for my share, I have found father Revel Sahib's medicine-box. Carrying this inheritance, I shall now embark on a path shown by brother Misir and seek my Ram. Pray, do not look for me.

Munshi Shivdharilal can be trusted to look after the estate. Should you need any more help, ask Registrar Sahib for it.

Wishing you good fortune

Having read the letter, Gulzaribai went numb. Bulakna was still waiting, his head still bowed. After a while, having regained her composure, she flounced indoors and returned quickly with a bag full of money. She gave it to Bulakna and said, 'Go, Bulakna, go. I relieve you of your duties. Go elsewhere, earn your livelihood, and live your life.'

Bulakna was tongue-tied. Clutching the bag of money, he waited for long in silence, his head bowed all the while. How could he look Gulzaribai in the face? Finally, he hobbled his way out of the mansion.

After seeing Bulakna off, she went straight to the White Mansion and collected the portraits of Revel Sahib and Haliwant Sahay—one from the shrine room and the other from the sitting room. Thereafter, she had its gate locked and returned to the Red Mansion. Apart from the gatekeepers, all other servants of the White Mansion were summoned for a farewell huddle. As salaries were being handed around, Gulzaribai burst into sobs and said, 'I feel crushed to let you all go.' But she had no choice. By now, the servants were also aware of the changed circumstances; there was no escaping the inevitable. They knew it well that when the sahib himself has abandoned his mansion, no one else could shelter them. Every one of them was in tears. Those golden days of abundance and joy, which they had spent in the sahib's company, were now behind them. Casting a final wistful glance at the White Mansion, they left for their homes.

Munshi Shivdharilal came running in. His face was wrinkled, but the gleam in his eyes was not lost. In spite of his advanced years, his tall and wiry frame was still in good shape. A knee-length dhoti, markeen kurta, traditional cap and a red towel slung across his shoulders—such was his customary attire. Holding on to Sahay's letter, he stood frozen for a long time. It had surely stirred a storm in his heart.

In terms of age, Sahay was much younger than Shivdharilal. He remembered how, years ago, when he had started working at Revel Sahib's bungalow, he was already past his youth, while Sahay was still poised on its threshold. Although he had come to him a broken man, Sahay had received him with bounteous affection. It was on the strength of that enveloping warmth that he had managed to survive, one day at a time. After a while, he wiped his eyes, cleared his throat and said, 'Babu Haliwant Sahay always took good care of me. Even in his retirement, he did not forget to provide for me; where else was I supposed to find refuge at this ripe old age? Bai-ji, I am ready to serve you. You shall be the mistress and I will be your servant. I will protect your wealth and carry out all your commands.'

Tears welled up in Gulzaribai's eyes. Forcing the bundle of documents in his hands, she said, 'No, Munshi-ji. I am not your mistress and you aren't my servant. You shall be my father and I will be your daughter.'

Overwhelmed with kindness, Shivdharilal chewed on his bottom lip, as he reflected on Gulzaribai's disarming words. Her noble gesture had left him dumbstruck.

* * *

When Rai Lachhman Prasad returned home from the law court and learnt of this sudden development, he was utterly shocked. Surely, he couldn't have foreseen the situation. He was very close to Sahay. On many occasions, he had gazed deep into Sahay's mind, and based on that, he could sense that Sahay was gradually becoming senile. Yet, his inventive mind had nurtured the hope that Sahay would do well to choose him as his heir. And in some remote recess of his head, he had also harboured tender feelings for Gulzaribai. As soon as he received the news of Sahay's departure, he lost no time in reaching the White Mansion. But its gate was locked. Upon seeing a friend of his former master, the gatekeeper broke down and wept inconsolably.

Prasad's entire body shook with anger and he stomped towards the Red Mansion. Gulzaribai's waiting-woman was standing at the gate. When she saw him approaching, with that look of fury on his face, she put herself across the gate and blocked his access. Irked by her impudence, he spoke to her in a domineering tone, trying to assert his authority, 'Listen, you! Go, inform Bai-ji at once.'

She did his bidding and returned almost immediately, with a somewhat discourteous message, 'Sahib, mistress is busy with her puja. It will be a while before she is ready to receive you.'

'Bai-ji is busy saying her prayers! Oh, really? Having killed seventy rats, the cat has become a saint,' he thought to himself.

The message sent by Gulzaribai burnt him up. Smarting under that lukewarm response, clearly intended as an insult, he left the scene right away. On his way back, he brooded over every possible strategy to meet the crisis at hand. 'That harlot Dhela rises to become the proprietor. All these years, I clung to Sahay as if I were his shadow. And what do I get? Well, so be it. If I am a true Kayasth, I'll reduce everything she owns to ashes.'

As soon as he reached home, his carriage was readied and he set out for Sheetlapur. The vehicle's sluggish pace on the muddy road caused him great annoyance. Every time he rebuked the carriage driver and grumbled about speed, the driver reacted by whipping the horse. It was only late at night that Prasad reached Sheetlapur, his head scheming furiously. A meeting with Sahay's relatives was promptly convened. Since it was already quite late, dinner was also served. They ate together and discussed strategies to do her out of her inheritance. An hour later, as the night deepened, Prasad set off for Chhapra. When his carriage drove past the Red Mansion, he turned to look at its high walls, a crooked smile playing on his face. 'So, is the saint still praying?' he thought to himself.

By afternoon, a small crowd had gathered near the White Mansion. Sahay's relatives were already there. Shivdharilal brought the keys and opened the gate. Putting down the documents for everyone to see, he started explaining everything in earnest, 'All you gentlemen are relatives of Sahib. I was only his humble servant. Since Sahib has forfeited everything, all of this is now yours.

If you find my services acceptable, you may employ me as a servant to look after this estate. What more can I say.'

One of Sahay's relative blared angrily, 'Munshi-ji, do not mislead us by feigning innocence. All these years, you duped and swindled our uncle; now, no more of your tricks. These papers that you have brought pertain only to half of his estate. Be a good man and bring the rest of the deeds, or unpleasant consequences are sure to follow.'

'Sahib, but the other half has been bequeathed to Gulzaribai. How am I supposed to give those papers to you?' he replied with utmost humility.

'By what right has our uncle given our ancestral property to a harlot? We are his legitimate heirs.'

That disrespectful remark incensed Munshi-ji. 'Son, mind your words,' saying so, he walked out of the White Mansion, even as the relatives looked on in surprise.

11

Friends, Foes and Heirs

When the night came, Prasad convened a meeting in the front yard of his house. The gates of the campus were shut to keep the affair guarded. Sahay's relatives had no idea about the extent of his wealth or the expanse of his estate. They never had the chance to enjoy proximity with him. Moreover, because of the social stigma that his decadent lifestyle carried, they usually stayed away from him. The unexpected windfall had driven them crazy, but they were furious because Gulzaribai was granted such a huge share in the property. 'Is that even lawful?' they asked Prasad and debated strategies to toss her out of the property-sharing arrangement. 'Is she a relation of Haliwant Sahay? What claim does that harlot have over his property?'

Prasad was delighted with the turn of events; he had found the strings that would let him manipulate them like puppets. But greed wasn't Prasad's only sin; he lusted for Gulzaribai too. For the past so many years, he had imagined himself to be the heir-apparent to everything that belonged to Sahay, including Gulzaribai. His mind obsessed over her beauty. However, with the changed circumstances, all his long-cherished plans were beginning to spin out of his control. Gulzaribai had become nearly inaccessible, as was half of Sahay's property that was bequeathed to her. And the other half, set aside for his relatives, was equally out-of-reach? But Prasad was a true Kayasth; he wasn't prepared to admit defeat without a fight.

Sahay's relatives lacked the means necessary for a long legal battle. But on the strength of Prasad's assurance of help, they decided to stay put in Chhapra and fight the lawsuit. Prasad was alert to their vulnerabilities, and too keen to exploit them. At the same time, he also wanted Gulzaribai to come running to him, and plead for rescue. Till that happened, he decided to wait in the wings, even as he pushed others to the centre stage.

'Please pay attention to my words. I am a government officer. I must not get embroiled in your messy property dispute. But it is no secret that Haliwant Sahay was my dearest friend. For that reason, I find it insufferable to live with the thought that a harlot might claim half of his wealth. Although, it is only fair that she, too, gets a little money to live on, but that does not mean she should end up owning half of his estate, in the same league as all you gentlemen. This is why I have decided to help you. You will find me standing with you at each step of the way. For your sake, I will even lobby judges and officials. But my name must never be mentioned. And yes, there is one more thing that you must keep in mind: sometimes, you might find Gulzaribai running to me for help, but you should not be worried by that. I am totally with you, body and spirit.'

Soon, preparations were afoot for fighting a legal battle and a lawsuit was duly filed. But the expenses of the court were steep, and the litigants were poor. From the very outset, Prasad started lending money to Sahay's relatives, just as he had promised. However, in public, he pretended to have little to do with the affair. When Gulzaribai got the legal notice, she called for Prasad, as was anticipated. Prasad was thrilled at the invitation, but he decided to conceal his elation and put on a look of nonchalance. When he reached the Red Mansion, he was given a warm welcome. It was the telltale sign that his scheme would bear fruits. Before long, Gulzaribai came out to meet him. She looked disturbed and jittery; one could sense that she was on the verge of breaking down. For Prasad, it was a supremely satisfying sight.

'Rai Sahib, what do you think of the court case? What will happen now?'

Prasad made a serious face and replied, 'Bai-ji, this lawsuit is as unpredictable as any other. At this point, I can't guess the outcome. But you don't need to worry.

I am here for you; you will always find me ready for any help that you might need.'

A little comforted, Gulzaribai continued, 'Munshi-ji told me that the very basis of the court case is flimsy. The relatives have no business questioning however Sahib decides to divide his property. Moreover, he hasn't so much as touched his ancestral deeds. He also said that since Sahib is still alive, these objections cannot be raised in the first place; as of now, they have no claim even on the share that has been set aside for them.'

'What else could one expect from Shivdharilal? The man has grown senile with age. Bai-ji, listen to me carefully. You must put up a strong defence in the law court. Also, you should not get complacent trusting that oldie. Your direct involvement in the matter is crucial. If you need any help, do not hesitate asking me for it. Yes?' Prasad could see that Gulzaribai was completely entangled in the trap he had laid out for her. Was it possible for her to escape? Where would the wild fox run to, if not to the wilderness? Satisfied at the way things were unfolding, he decided to leave, lest his exhilaration should become apparent to his host. He was truly on cloud nine.

* * *

When the vagaries of life make humans fearful, their hearts turn to deities and ancestors for comfort. Gulzaribai's condition was no different. Not too long ago, she enjoyed

a patronage so bounteous and steady that the cares of the
world were not for her. But soon, everything went topsy-
turvy, almost without a warning. All of a sudden, she
found herself burdened with the responsibilities of a huge
estate. And the lawsuit, which questioned her rights over
that very estate, followed soon afterwards. For Gulzaribai,
these were troubled times. All through the day, she would
juggle the affairs of the zamindari and visits to the lawyer.
It was only in the shrine room that she found a little
solace. Meanwhile, Mahendar was called upon to restart
the tradition of late-evening devotional recitals. Every day,
he would serenade his audience with his velvety voice,
new compositions and inventive tunes. People held him
in high esteem and Gulzaribai saw to it that all his needs
were taken care of.

Sometimes, during those moments of tranquility in
the shrine room, she would sing a snatch from one of his
songs. When her placid voice reached Mahendar, piercing
through the high walls of the Red Mansion, he would
feel himself grow extremely restless. And whenever that
happened, Gulzaribai's nose ring, which always remained
in his pocket, appeared to flare up. Choked on his own
baffling sentiments, Mahendar would simply pace about
his room.

With each passing day, the court case was getting more
and more knotty, as all such cases are known to get. And
as the legal process unfolded, Prasad became increasingly
indispensable. With great cunning, he managed to appear

loyal to both the parties; the new owners of the White Mansion were totally dependent on him for monetary assistance, while Gulzaribai put all her faith in his legal advice. To both of them, he was not just their greatest sympathizer, but their chief counselor too.

Before long, Prasad became a regular visitor to the Red Mansion. Whenever he came over, he was received with elaborate rites of hospitality; the servants were prompt in attending to all his comforts and he was treated to a variety of expensive foreign wines. But in spite all the ceremonies of affection, Gulzaribai, for her part, remained somewhat distant from him. Prasad found her willed detachment unbearable, yet, like an expert hunter, he remained on the lookout for every opportune moment. For many reasons, Shivdharilal did not quite approve of him. But the worldly-wise old hand chose to remain tight-lipped about it; he was gripped by the realization that since he was a mere servant of the mansion, he must refrain from sticking his nose in the affairs of his employer.

Like Shivdharilal, Mahendar, too, disliked Prasad. In fact, he loathed his intimate overtures towards Gulzaribai. He felt that Prasad's daily visits somehow diminished him. Was he not the man in the house? Whenever those visits coincided with his performance, he grew so nervy that his singing went out of tune and he started forgetting the lyrics of his own composition. He often wondered why Gulzaribai had to treat Prasad with such excessive warmth; must he enjoy all those liberties in the Red Mansion? Every time these thoughts crossed his mind, he could feel the piercing presence of Gulzaribai's nose ring more keenly.

Soon, Gulzaribai started consulting a lawyer and a tiring routine of visits to his office commenced. Everyday, she would climb into her carriage and set off for the lawyer's place. During such visits, she was often escorted by Prasad. To Mahendar, this was an insufferable sight. With each passing day, his restlessness grew. And then, one day, when he could no longer hold that deluge of emotions, he decided to confront her.

It was nearing sunset. Gulzaribai was getting ready to visit her lawyer, and as always, Prasad was to accompany her. A carriage awaited them on the porch. As Gulzaribai approached the vehicle, Mahendar blocked her way and said, 'There is something that I need to tell you.'

'Please do.'

'Not here. I'll speak to you alone.'

Gulzaribai was visibly irked by the suggestion; for a while, she just stared at him. 'All right, once I come back to the mansion, I'll hear you out,' she said, with her brows arched, and her tone solemn. And then, she hopped into the carriage, as did Prasad. The vehicle moved out of the gate, making a rhythmic 'tik tik' sound.

Mahendar was taken aback by her snub; it took him a while to regain his nerves. He could feel blood rush to his head and his entire body shook. He stepped out of the mansion, hoping to escape this feeling of humiliation. As he walked along the river, the cold breeze that blew over the Saryu brought him a little respite. Yet, his heart raced whenever he thought of the episode. When nothing seemed to bring him comfort, he returned to his room, tumbled into his bed and dozed off.

He was in a quandary; time and again, he regretted his decision to face up to Gulzaribai, but her nose ring ignited a feeling of envy towards Prasad. He felt that he was being slighted on purpose, so that Prasad may feel valued. How come Gulzaribai had no time for him? Humbled by the stinging insult, he kept telling himself that he never should have meddled in the personal affairs of those around him. After much soul-searching, he decided that he would neither breathe a word of what had happened, nor would he broach the subject ever again. But Gulzaribai's ever-growing closeness with Prasad made him green with envy, and the nose ring in his pocket convinced him that he was free to bare his heart to her.

When Tiwari-ji woke him up at dinner time, he obliged him by eating a little, albeit disinterestedly. A weird and uneasy feeling had overtaken him. He was unable to extricate himself from that long-drawn-out dilemma. Feeling sorry for himself, he crashed again on his bed and soon, fell asleep.

Around midnight, Gulzaribai's carriage rumbled back into the mansion. When Mahendar heard that noise, his heart started pounding. The carriage stopped briefly on the porch, and then proceeded towards the garage. Once again, all was quiet. Mahendar breathed a sigh of relief. But barely fifteen minutes had passed when a servant arrived to summon him, 'Misir Baba, are you asleep? Please come with me, the mistress calls you.'

The unexpected summon had put Mahendar in a dilemma. Should he snub her back by pretending to be asleep, or should he oblige her? But all his conundrum aside, he was sure of the nose ring; it reminded him of his rights in the Red Mansion. Buoyed by the thought, he decided to accompany the messenger.

Gulzaribai was waiting for him in the sitting room, sunk in a couch. She was quiet and still. Her beauty, like flames against a dark night, shone brighter under the faint light of the lamp. As Mahendar stepped inside the room, he couldn't escape being scorched by that flame. She signaled him to sit on the couch opposite hers. He could feel that her composure was insincere. Since their earlier interaction, Mahendar's own keenness to discuss the matter had simmered down very much. And now, having seen that look of uneasy calm on her face, he felt all the more hesitant.

'Misir-ji, you wanted to say something in private. Well, go ahead,' Gulzaribai breached that uncomfortable silence.

Mahendar found her candor quite surprising. He couldn't bring himself to utter a word of the speech he had been rehearsing in his head. Gulzaribai frowned at his silence. That stern look unsettled him further and he felt a sudden rush of blood. Clearing his throat, he blurted everything out at one go.

'I wanted to say that Lachhman Babu isn't a good man. Spending too much of your time with him would be unwise.'

Gulzaribai straightened her back, sat upright, and stared at him coldly. Then, in a grave voice, she said, 'Misir-ji, I am not a child who needs to be told good from bad. I will do whatever I consider right and proper. I will make friends with whoever I wish to get friendly with. Who are you to place restrictions on me? What right do you have to interfere in my affairs? Also, I want you to get this straight: I am not a petty-minded person like you. Before you set out to sermonize, please be advised to look at your own conduct.'

* * *

Mahendar stood stunned by that response, unable to believe his ears. So searing were her words that he felt as if someone had poured molten glass straight into his eardrums. His throat went dry. All of his agitation and envy had evaporated in the space of a few moments. He pictured himself in free fall, plummeting to his certain demise, with no one to rescue him.

'O' God, what just happened? O' what have you done, Mahendar?'

He was at his wit's end; he didn't know how to react to that terrible insult. Faced with that impossible quandary, he unmindfully slid his hands into the pockets of his coat and sat motionless in intense embarrassment. The packet containing Gulzaribai's nose ring was still there. When he felt it with his fingers, he pulled it out, and for a while, kept tossing it about—from one hand to another. Once his throbbing head had cooled down, he put it on the centre-table and got up to leave. Gulzaribai's couch was lying vacant. As he stepped out of the sitting room, recalling the scene that had just ended, he could not stop cursing himself.

'O' Ram, how did all this happen? Why did I lose my mind?'

His world had been turned upside down; one moment, he was flying high in the sky, the next moment, he had sunk into a dark pit within the earth. He had finally awakened to the seamy side of life and his natural simplicity was corroded. That onerous shame threatened to bury him under its own weight. He stepped out of the mansion and stopped for a while on the porch. The ground beneath his feet felt like embers and the place had become insufferable. Instead of returning to his room, he headed out of the gate and kept walking frantically. Bursting with regret, he merely followed his feet and went in whatever direction they took him. He was too mortified to cast even one last glance at the Red Mansion.

When he composed himself, he realized that he was standing at the Chhapra station. A train was waiting on the platform. For a while, he just stood there, in a state of indecision. The train whistled and its compartments began to move. As the last compartment was about to trundle past him, he hopped in unthinkingly. The train sped off.

12

A Brief Stopover

By the time the train reached Banaras City, it was already afternoon. Mahendar looked listless and sad. Taking pity on him, a concerned co-passenger decided to offer a practical advice and said, 'Baba, why don't you alight here itself, instead of the going to the next station? The next stop is a major junction. They might catch you there. I can see that you are travelling without a ticket, aren't you?'

Mahendar heeded the advice. Once he got down, that very co-passenger had another suggestion: he asked him to wait on the platform till the crowd dispersed. It took barely two minutes for the crowd to thin out. Soon the stationmaster ended his watch at the exit gate and strolled back to his office. Sensing an opportunity, he slipped out of the railway station.

The place was totally unfamiliar. There were no acquaintances either. He loitered about the city, a pain searing in his heart. His savings were so meager that living in Banaras was sure to prove extremely challenging. Where to rest, where to go, he was without a clue.

He wandered aimlessly for the whole day, and when evening came, he found himself at the famous Dashaswamegh ghat. The soothing sight of the Ganga-ji brought a sense of calm. He plunged in the cool water of the river and feeling somewhat rejuvenated, settled on the steps of the ghat. As he sat there, quietly idling his time away, evening gave way to night, but the crowd kept surging. It was the day of the Budhwa Mangal fair and the entire city had converged on the ghat. As far as the eyes could see, spectacularly bedecked houseboats floated all over the Ganga-ji's bosom. And each of these houseboats hosted private mehfils of the patricians of Banaras. It appeared as if the kingdom of Indra, with all its divine opulence, had descended on the earth.

On one of the houseboats he spotted Vidyadharibai. And then, on a second, he saw Kesarbai. There were so many of those dazzling houseboats, and each played host to a famous tawaif of Banaras. How was he supposed to recognize all of them? As he stood mesmerized by the grandeur of the night, someone thrust a plate of pooris in his hand. He had been starving since morning; that toothsome fragrance of ghee was all the joy his heart craved for at the moment. How could anyone starve in this great city of Annapurna, the presiding deity of plentitude?

By morning, the festivities of the Budhwa Mangal were over, but Mahendar stayed on. He had found a permanent refuge on the ghat. Thenceforth, he would roam around the city all day long, and once it got dark, he would return to the ghat and sleep on its broad steps.

* * *

One day, as he was sitting purposelessly on the ghat, he reached into his pocket, perhaps out of habit. But there was nothing to be found. His empty pocket prompted him to reflect on how, until that unfortunate night, he had always treasured Gulzaribai's nose ring. But, consumed by shame, he had abandoned it on a table and walked away from it, with no regrets whatsoever. Indeed, this is what saint Kabir meant when he said, 'At the journey's end, I surrendered my shawl, in the same form that I had found it.' Mahendar felt a sudden urge to sing and started crooning one of his own old compositions.

'O' beloved,
As I kneaded your head,
Shoved by your elbow,
My nose ring got mislaid.'

There was a small temple dedicated to the goddess Annapurna, not too far from the spot on the ghat where Mahendar usually lazed about. That day, as Kesarbai was stepping out of that temple, she heard the words of a memorable song, sung in a fairly familiar voice. As she turned back elatedly, looking for the source of that unforgettable melody, her eyes fell on Mahendar. He was sitting right ahead of her, completely engrossed in his music. She hurried to greet him, but decided to wait for the song to end. Once it came to a close and Mahendar opened his eyes, she exclaimed, 'Misir-ji, what brings you . . . ?'

Mahendar had a nodding acquaintance with Kesarbai. On a few occasions, he had seen her at the Red Mansion in Chhapra. The moment he recognized her, he respectfully rose to his feet, but chose not to say anything in reply. His face appeared parched and sad. Kesarbai could read his situation.

'Misir-ji, when did you come to Banaras?' she asked.

'Well, four or five days ago.'

'And where are you staying, Misir-ji?'

Mahendar had no answer to her question. After a moment of silence, he looked up and replied in an impassive tone, 'I stay in the company of my body.'

Kesarbai looked at him intently, smiled and said, 'In that case, allow me invite you to my place. Please come with me.'

Indeed, a drowning man will clutch at a straw; homeless for days, Mahendar could not decline the offer and followed her in silence. Soon, the two reached Dalmandi, the notorious neighborhood of the tawaifs of Banaras. Mahendar was quite fascinated by the rows of glittering shops that sat pompously on either side of the narrow lane. Kesarbai directed him to a stairway which stood huddled between two shops and led to the first floor of a rickety building. Mahendar obliged and climbed up the steps unthinkingly. However, once he reached the doorway, he was astonished to find that a house, which appeared so gloomy from the outside, had such ornate interiors; it was nearly as stunning as its owner.

Kesarbai had keen eyes. With a simple glance, she could easily guess what a patron was worth. It took her no time to figure out Mahendar's condition; that he was completely helpless became instantly obvious to her. It was this remarkable gift of observation that had aided her numerous conquests as a tawaif. Today, however, it was of no use to her. To every question that she could possibly ask, there was only one invariable response: silence.

* * *

In the heart of hearts, Kesarbai nurtured a monumental ambition. She longed to surpass Vidyadharibai's musical abilities and outshine her. To this end, she had trained under several renowned gurus. Yet, she could not achieve total mastery over the elusive rasas. Although she was quite aware of Pandit Ramnarayan Misir's high reputation as a singer, and on a few occasions, she had even heard him sing, but by then, Ramnarayan had restricted himself to only devotional compositions. However, Mahendar, his disciple, was in the prime of his musical prowess. When Kesarbai had first heard his voice at Haliwant Sahay's durbar in Chhapra, she was awestruck and quick to conclude that if the celestial ambrosia indeed existed in the world, it had to be found in Mahendar's throat. Today, when that same person stood before her in flesh and blood, she felt that all her prayers have been answered and an omniscient God had quietly created a golden opportunity for her; on the auspicious the day of the goddess Annapurna—the deity had blessed her with a mentor who would help her accomplish her long-standing personal quest. Putting the ceremonial platter away, she turned to Mahendar and pleaded, 'Misir-ji, where would you go, leaving behind this city of Lord Vishwanath and goddess Annapurna? Stay here and accept me as your disciple.' Mahendar's silence indicated his consent.

Soon arrangements were made for his stay at Kesarbai's Chetgunj mansion. Mahendar started living by a strict routine, leaving days of vagrancy behind him. He would wake up before dawn, bathe in the Ganga-ji, offer water as oblation at the Vishwanath temple and then, proceed quickly to Kesarbai's nautch-house to supervise her morning practice of poorvi songs. Thereafter, for the rest of the day, he would focus on his own music and sing for hours to hone his skills. When evening fell, he would go to Kabir Chaura, a locality famous for the musicians of the Misir clan. He greatly relished the pleasant company of his fellow musicians; sitting in their midst, he would sing merrily and gossip till late. In no time, Mahendar's reputation as an exceptionally gifted singer grew manifold and he became the golden boy of Banaras. He was invited to perform at the grandest of durbars in the city. Respect and money, both started pouring in aplenty.

* * *

Kesarbai was that maddening fragrance whose mere presence could intoxicate a mehfil. She was much like a diamond, both brilliant and lethal. With the help of her anklet bells and her astonishingly nimble feet, she could imitate every subtle beat produced on a tabla. To top it all, she was blessed with a honeyed voice. No matter which mehfil she performed at, she always had her audience in her thrall. But in spite of all her feats, she nursed a secret sorrow: she could never bring herself to compete against Vidyadharibai at the Budhwa Mangal fair. Under the circumstances, Mahendar appeared as a charm that could magically bridge the gulf separating the two. In months that followed, Kesarbai devoted herself to the universe of poorvi songs and drank deeply at the springs of its sentimental poetry and melodious tunes. Each dawn, as Mahendar arrived to train her, she received him with utmost respect and great eagerness to perfect her craft. However, Mahendar experienced an intense attraction to her. Whenever he saw Kesarbai's face, Gulzaribai's radiant image flashed before his mind. And the strain of melancholy, always so evident in his songs, deepened further. As days went by, his longing for Kesarbai intensified; whether asleep or awake, he dreamt of her all the time. And then, one day, calamity struck.

It was already past the first watch of the night. Mahendar was getting ready to leave the impromptu singing contest at Kabir Chaura. Just then, he had a surreal sensation; he was so overwhelmed by a particular song that he felt as if he could actually taste its rasa—a taste as overpowering as the intoxicating scent that came from Kesarbai's body. Once he was reminded of her, his feet started moving towards Dalmandi, quite involuntarily.

The mehfils of that infamous address were beginning to peak and the air around the nautch-houses was itself filled with sweet music. Mahendar was quick to climb the steps that led to Kesarbai's nautch-house. His unexpected arrival at an odd hour took the doorman by surprise. Obstructing his passage, he alerted him with utmost courtesy. 'Baba, Raja Sahib has come.'

But he did not pay any attention to those words of caution and rushed to the doorway, his reason blurred by lust. The mehfil was in full swing; one could hear the rhythmic beats of the tabla and the resonant harmony of the sarangi. Inside the nautch-house, Raja Sahib sat reclining against a bolster. Attired in a richly embroidered *achkan,* he glittered like gold. And expensive red wine swirled in the delicately-carved cup that he held in his hand. But Kesarbai's seductive beauty was more potent than any

intoxicant. When she drew near Raja Sahib, he gently held
her chin and stared deep into her eyes.

> 'Who would calm the ache in my heart, O' Rama?
> Who would cure my poisoned body?
> O' sister-in-law,
> Pray, light the lamp.'

Her song had the qualities of both fire and poison; it
could burn, it could kill. Having witnessed that scene,
Mahendar's euphoria evaporated. When Kesarbai noticed
him, she rose to her feet with sensual frolic, picked up a
jug of wine, poured some more in Raja Sahib's cup and
advanced towards the door, cleverly maneuvering the steps
of her dance arrangement. By then, her accompanist had
started improvising the song's refrain on sarangi, and Raja
Sahib had raised the replenished cup to his lips, ready for
another swig. Sensing an opportunity, Kesarbai clutched
the door and spoke chidingly to Mahendar, 'Misir-ji, you
have no sense of time or occasion. You must go away.'
Having issued a quick rebuke, she swirled back towards
Raja Sahib.

Mahendar froze. Kesarbai's shameless coquetry in
the presence of another man had left him shattered. That
seductive body and its intoxicating fragrance, which had
drawn him to Dalmandi, now emitted an appalling stench.
The blistering insult, which Kesarbai had inflicted on him,
hurt even more under the flames of envy. His feeling of

humiliation was so brutal that he felt as if Kesarbai had spat on his face.

He hastened downstairs and dashed towards his residence. Reaching Chetgunj, he counted his savings, picked up a few clothes and stormed out of the mansion. From there, he walked straight to the station and waited on the platform for the train to Chhapra. But he found himself haunted by those two faces; memories of both Kesarbai and Dhelabai floated in his mind and refused to let go of their hold on him. For Mahendar, those faces were knotted with painful tales of humiliation. However, much as he wanted to, he could not blank them out.

'O' Ram, where shall I go?'

Just then, the passenger ahead of him at the ticket counter hurriedly demanded a ticket to the Howrah-bound train. With the same urgency, he, too, held out money for a ticket to Howrah.

13

The Forgotten Ones

For three consecutive days, as the lawsuit was being put to trail, Gulzaribai had become completely oblivious to the world beyond the court. In the midst of that constant scuttling between the court and the lawyer's office, where was the time to pay attention to other things. And whenever she returned to her mansion to get some sleep, exhausted though she was, anxiety kept her open-eyed through the night. Food or rest, nothing seemed to matter to her.

Finally, the verdict was delivered; Gulzaribai won the legal battle. Riding a carriage and flanked by her supporters, she set out triumphantly for her mansion. A band of musicians marched ahead of her vehicle, leading the victory procession. Once she reached home, she was besieged by elated friends and swarmed with the congratulatory messages. The day was long and eventful. Exhausted at the end, she plopped down into the couch placed in the sitting room. The servants were jubilant and hundreds had thronged to the mansion, asking for baksheesh and celebratory savories.

In the middle of these celebrations, Gulzaribai noticed a tiny paper-packet lying neglected on the table. Engrossed in a jovial gossip with friends and well-wishers, she picked it up distractedly. For a while, as the chit-chat continued, she kept tossing it about, from her left hand to her right. A few tosses later, as the paper dampened with the sweat in her palm, the packet started to wither at the edges and its folds loosened.

At first, she suspected it to be something small and globular, but when she opened the packet and studied the object, she was deeply hurt by her discovery. An unspoken agony pierced her bosom. The glittering nose ring that she held in her palm triggered a surge of emotion. She thought of her own identity and her forgotten past; the pain had awakened her to her long-subdued womanhood. Stirred by the find, she got up at once, rushed indoors and called out to her waiting woman, 'Sanichari, go fetch Misir-ji.'

Sanichari snapped at Gulzaribai, waving her hands vigorously in irritation, 'At this odd hour, wherever would you find Misir-ji? Dear Madam, he has been absconding for some days past. He must be too busy leading the life of a vagrant, eh!'

'Hold your tongue!' Gulzaribai retorted. However, the thought of Mahendar's disappearance made her dizzy and an ominous darkness began to engulf her. With all her strength, she squeezed at the ring. A little later, once she regained her composure, she dragged herself to her bedroom and crashed on the bed.

As soon as Prasad returned from work, he headed straight to the Red Mansion to congratulate Gulzaribai. But he was stopped on the porch by a waiting woman who told him that the mistress was a bit under the weather, and therefore, unavailable to meet anyone. Lachhman Prasad got the message. Inflamed by the insult it concealed, he retreated to his place, seething with anger. All of the Red Mansion was wrapped in a festive mood. Ecstatic servants spent the entire night rejoicing and singing verses from the Ramayana.

* * *

When morning dawned, men were sent in all directions to look for Mahendar. Every lane of Mishrawaliya, Pakadi and Revelgunj was thoroughly searched, yet no clue was found of his whereabouts. Gulzaribai felt miserable. She lay grief-stricken on her bed, her face buried in the pillow. Shivdharilal scratched his head, feeling both helpless and stumped. How very reckless the ways of youth are, he thought. His own story was no different. Years ago, it was in a fit of youthful rage that he had arrived at the doorsteps of the Opium Bungalow. He waited by Gulzaribai's bed, and after a while, quietly slipped out of her room.

It wasn't difficult for Shivdharilal to guess what had happened. He had swallowed many bitter pills himself and those distressing experiences had made him worldly-wise. He did know a thing or two about a woman's heart. He knew it well that a woman's passion cares little for the ways of the world; it thrives undeterred by social mores. A man, by contrast, has little choice in these matters. He is expected to weather by himself every storm that rages in his heart. Even if his soul gets gashed and shredded, he must appear unruffled to the world. This everlasting struggle against one's own self is every man's painful fate.

Whenever Shivdharilal saw Gulzaribai, he was reminded of his second wife. He had married her after the death of the first. His first wife could not bear him a child. Although the second wife gave him a son, she could never find a way into his heart. It was a disastrous match. Shortly after he became a father, she abandoned her infant son and decamped with a boy from their neighborhood. Even though it happened ages ago, Shivdharilal still squirmed with embarrassment at the thought of it. The day he had learnt of her treachery, he had picked up his son, and in the dark of the night, left his home for good. How very desperate he was to erase his identity, to forget that he was Shankar Prasad from . . .

Adopting the name Shivdharilal, he landed a job in the Opium Bungalow and started raising his son. But Shivratan seemed to have taken after his mother. Before he came of age, he fled to Calcutta with Ganeshiya—the married daughter of a maid at the Opium Bungalow. Embarrassed again, Shivdharilal wanted to run away to anonymity. However, since he was well along in years and lacked the raw audacity that comes with youth, he had to abandon that idea. Somehow, he always felt that Sahay had an inkling of his compulsions.

There were times when Gulzaribai's striking beauty caused him a little unease. It brought back to him the loveliness and the charms of his second wife. He had experienced a similar restlessness the day when Meenabai had left for Muzaffarpur, leaving everyone puzzled by the suddenness of her departure. That day, before announcing her resolve to return to her city, she had cast inquisitive glances at Shivdharilal. Subjected to her probing gaze, Shivdharilal had felt an intense agitation.

* * *

Gulzaribai's lotus eyes looked bloodshot and swollen.

'Munshi-ji,' she called out.

Shivdharilal was distracted by the string of memories that flowed through his mind, but her voice pulled him back to the here and now.

'Munshi-ji, you must make arrangements for a more thorough search.'

'All possible arrangements have already been made, Bai-ji. I'll keep a close watch on everything myself. You should rest assured.'

The search went on for several days, but Mahendar remained untraceable. Meanwhile, Prasad's patience began to wear off. Each day he visited the Red Mansion, wanting nothing less than Gulzaribai's personal attention. He tried hard to draw her into lighthearted gossips and soften her up till she came under this thumb. However, contrary to his mighty hopes, he ended up feeling tormented by her never-ending discussions about Mahendar. It is indeed profoundly excruciating for any man to sustain his patience when a beautiful woman speaks obsessively of another man. But the seasoned Prasad endured this too. He tried every trick that he had up his sleeves, yet Gulzaribai kept slipping away. Sometimes, in a desperate bid to impress her with the sincerity of his friendship, he even faked concern Mahendar and grilled Shivdharilal about the progress of the search operation in her presence.

But Shivdharilal was disapproving of the entire hullabaloo around the disappearance of a jilted man. Years ago, when his wife had run away, he had made no effort to trace her. Later, when his son eloped, he once again decided against putting himself under any unnecessary stress. Must he strive so hard to search for a man who doesn't have anyone to call his own?

This debate caused him great unease. Once he had seen a strange dream: he saw that the boy his wife had fled away with had deserted her, and in the ensuing tumult, he was left with no strength in his body to run to her rescue. This bizarre vision haunted him for long afterwards. However, things simmered down gradually, and the burden of estate management obliged him to let go of the bygones.

Several years had passed since Shivdharilal's son had fled Chhapra. The fact that Shivratan had a settled way of life in Calcutta was all the consolation he needed to live his life in peace. Once in a while, the news of his son's well being trickled to him. Sometimes, he even received clothes and gifts sent from Calcutta. Whenever that happened, he did not forget to thank the gods and extol his good fortune. Meanwhile, with each passing day, Prasad kept getting more and more impatient. Whenever Shivdharilal saw him, he was reminded of his own son. He feared that just as Shivratan had run away with Ganeshiya, Prasad, too, will decamp with Gulzaribai soon. Shivdharilal often likened him to a sly wild cat; one that crouches with infinite patience and stuns its prey at an opportune moment. His vastly experienced eyes told him that Prasad was after Gulzaribai's wealth—her mansion and her estate. Like a vigilant cobra that guards its burrow, he remained sharp and watchful.

But, one day, the entire Red Mansion erupted with disbelief. People were shocked to learn that Prasad had furtively grabbed the White Mansion—one of Sahay's most prized possessions. The relatives of Sahay could do nothing about it. During that long-drawn-out property dispute, he had not only provided them money to meet the expenses of the law court, but had also goaded them to pursue the lawsuit till the bitter end. However, now that the court case was lost and their resources drained, there was no question of them repaying their debts. Preying on their helplessness, he had succeeded in grabbing the White Mansion—something he always coveted. Later that day, when he visited the Red Mansion to offer an explanation for his actions, a livid Gulzaribai insulted him and had him thrown out of the premises. 'I cannot suffer the sight of this wretched sinner,' she lashed out at him. Taken aback by her angry outburst, Prasad slunk out of the campus, red-faced

The news sunk Shivdharilal. Although the episode had exposed Prasad's true character and alerted Gulzaribai to her potential enemies, but he considered it a moment of colossal personal failure; he was trumped by the cunning of the world. He really took it to heart and was so severely affected by it that he soon fell ill. When Shivratan was informed of his father's poor health, he returned to Chhapra to nurse him. This was his first visit to the town since he had eloped with Ganeshiya. By the time he reached, Shivdharilal had grown too feeble to even speak. But during his final moments, when Shivratan tried to pour a driblet of water from the sacred Ganga-ji into his mouth, he somehow found the strength to holdout his hand in protest and stopped him from performing that ritual. Yet, days later, the same son lit his funeral pyre. The departed soul had no choice in the matter. Such is the lot of a dead man! They have no right over their own remains, no care for honor or shame. On the thirteenth day, once all the rites were observed, Shivratan left for Calcutta.

* * *

Without Shivdharilal, Gulzaribai was at a loss to order the affairs of the estate. She felt lonely too. The White Mansion scam had laid bare the avaricious schemes of Prasad. There was now no one whom she could trust. Like a fish stranded on land that gasps for breath, she groped around desperately for support and sympathy. She meditated for hours, sitting in front of Revel Sahib's portrait, but the Sahib did not speak to her. She even lit candles and prayed at his grave, yet the road ahead looked dark as ever. One day, after a trip to Revelgunj, as she rode back to the mansion, she noticed a boy of fourteen or fifteen standing on the steps near the porch. Although his hair was cropped and his tattered clothes were soiled, his faced looked handsome. He was waiting for her with folded hands, wearing a look of anxiety on his face.

'Who are you, son?' she asked.

'I am the grandson of Babu Gurbachan Sahay, Babu Haliwant Sahay's cousin,' he replied, respectfully.

For someone who was so maliciously harassed by the relatives of Haliwant Sahay, the mere mention of their names was enough to provoke a fit of anger. But she could not place Gurbachan Sahay; his name was never mentioned during the court case.

Restraining herself with much effort, she asked, 'Where do you come from? Sheetlapur?'

'No, mistress, I am from Gunzarawala in Punjab.'

'From Gunzarawala? Punjab?

'Yes mistress. My great-grandfather had migrated to that place. A few weeks ago, I lost my entire family to the plague epidemic in Punjab. I am the only survivor. Shortly before dying, my grandfather had asked me to come to Chhapra and seek shelter with his younger cousin, Babu Haliwant Sahay. But now that I am here, having discharged all my sacred duties towards the dead, I am told that my grand-uncle has left everything to become a monk. I know no one here. Where can I go?' By the time he finished speaking, he was choked and tears welled up in his eyes.

Moved by the boy's tragic story, she wept with him too. Steadying herself, she walked up to him, and with the aanchal of her sari, wiped off the tears from his eyes, and hers.

'Don't cry, son. I am your grand-aunt. I will take care of you,' she said, with loving tenderness.

To Ramprasad, it was like finding a harbour in the middle of a raging tempest.

14

The Past and the Future

Even though Calcutta was vast and unfamiliar, Mahendar had no reason to panic since his bag was swollen with cash. During his early days in Banaras, his challenges were twice as big: the place was unfamiliar to him and he was a pauper. If he could tough it out there, why should life in Calcutta present greater difficulties? After getting off the train at Howrah, he rented a room at a dharmashala and went sightseeing across the city. The majestic buildings of Calcutta were so tall that if a man tilted his head upwards to form an idea of their height, his turban would fall off his head. Every now and then, a tram would trundle by, rolling over the narrow rails laid out on the city's tidy graveled roads. Mahendar was totally awestruck by the ease with which the massive tramcars glided along the winding tracks. And when night came, his sense of wonder deepened. The gas lamps that lit up the streets of Calcutta could easily rival daylight. Never before in his life had he seen things so luminous. Indeed, the blazing torches of Banaras and Chhapra were no match. He had heard people say that Calcutta never goes to sleep. True to the legend, Mahendar found the city wide awake. He loitered around till late into the night and returned to his room only after fatigue got the better of his desire to explore the city further.

But Calcutta was a metropolitan city. His daily expenses increased considerably, and in no time, he found himself short of money. Besides, the solitary life was too oppressive a burden to bear. To escape this tedium, Mahendar thought of seeking work. His strong body and tall frame proved quite helpful in this pursuit. Within a few days, he got employed as a gatekeeper with Harrison & Company, a Bowbazar-based firm that sold gas lamps. The company provided him with a room in the same locality, and before long, his life fell into a new routine. At the end of each day, as he walked back to his room for the night, the abject loneliness which defined his life in the new city tore open old sores. And the wounds he had borne during his days in Chhapra and Banaras started bleeding again. In these troubled hours, he would, quite involuntarily, seek comfort in music and start singing.

* * *

One day, as he was relaxing in his room, singing a snatch from a plaintive poorvi, someone knocked on the door.

'I was a sprightly fish in a pond, O' Madhav,
You turned me into a vagabond.
I left my family; I left my home, O' Madhav,
You turned me into a vagabond.'

That noise broke his trance. As he opened the door, he saw a young Bengali lady standing outside his room. Her complexion was dusky, her body was voluptuous and her curly hair were neatly tied in a bun-shaped hairdo. She looked Mahendar up and down with her big impish eyes and teased him with mock complain in Bengali-mixed Hindustani. 'Mr Gatekeeper, why are you keen on slaying me with your songs?'

Mahendar felt awed by the beauty of his unexpected guest and her startling overtures. His mind went blank.

'I know what assails your heart. Come, let me cure your malady,' she added and clutched his hand. As she led him on, a hypnotized Mahendar followed her unthinkingly, without uttering a word. Long after his days of dalliance with Gulzari and Kesar, the seductive scent of a woman had once again made him restive. He was taken to a dingy room in the adjacent lane, right across his own room. Once inside, they settled on a rug. Every aspect of her being— her sheer beauty, her body, her bewitching laughter and her breath—oozed lust and desire. She poured alcohol into two cups, held out one to Mahendar, and said laughing, 'Here, drink this, the medicine for all your sufferings. If you fancy surviving this heartless world, I suggest you develop a taste for this potion.'

But Mahendar did not flinch. He was too mesmerized to notice the cup in her outstretched hand, his eyes feasting on the charms of his hostess. Finding him lost and dumbstruck, she playfully brought the cup to his lips. Mahendar did not resist the offering; he drank it greedily, emptying the cup in a gulp.

'Look, my name is Manorama. I thrive in the hearts of men. And the men . . . well, they come to me, seeking balsam for their scorched souls. Do you get me?' As she uttered those words, her eyes lit up and a mischievous smile played on her face.

Mahendar stared at her for long, admiring every little detail of her appearance: her dusky complexion, her luscious body, her big refulgent eyes and the bold crimson dot on her broad forehead. But more than everything else, it was the heady fragrance of a woman's body that intensified his longing. And as his inebriation deepened, so did his ecstasy, till he was completely drowned in alcohol.

Next morning, when he opened his eyes, Manorama was still asleep. She lay curled on the rag, carefree and with her clothes disheveled. He stood up hurriedly and got ready to leave. But barely had he reached the door when Manorama opened her eyes. Arching her body languidly, she smiled and said, 'Misir-ji, there stretches another day, to be spent battling sorrows of life.'

Mahendar spent his entire day regretting events of the previous night. He tried his best to put his heart into his work. However, once it got dark, he found himself irresistibly drawn to Manorama's room. And then, the same alcohol, the same insobriety—thus ended another night, battling the same old sorrows. Soon this became a routine of sorts. Night after night, one night at a time, the two waged incessant battle against the miseries of life.

However, one evening, not too long after this daily rite had commenced, Mahendar's newfound way of coping with life got rudely interrupted when he found a lock hung on Manorama's door. For the rest of the night, he kept circling her place, agitated and aching for her. The next evening brought no respite either. Seeing the lock dangle in the same position, his anger blazed up uncontrollably. In a fury, he kicked the door, stomped out of her lane and stormed towards the liquor shop. Just as he was beginning to descend the steps of the shop, having bought a bottle of alcohol, he was intercepted midway by a stranger. 'Misir Baba, is that you?'

A strange sensation ran through his body. He was surprised to notice that a thoroughly Bengali-looking man, in a totally unfamiliar city, had addressed him as if he was a close acquaintance. There was indeed an air of familiarity about him. Wherever could he have seen him? As he strained his memory a little, he could now easily place him, in spite the new appearance that the stranger had put on. 'Arrey Bulakna! What on earth are you doing here?' he nearly shrieked in surprise.

'Baba, please do not be so loud. We aren't too far from each other, are we? I can hear you well enough,' said Bulakna and broke into a guffaw.

Bulakna was quick to ask him over to his place. Mahendar happily obliged, and soon, the two started walking towards Bulakna's home.

'Baba, there is something I must tell you. Over here, no one has heard of Bulakna Dom. They know me as Bulaki Lal Kayath. Please be a little discreet when my Bengali wife is around,' Bulakna requested.

The revelation produced another shock on a day full of surprises. When Bulakna had left Chhapra, he had plenty of money with him. Undoubtedly, it was the availability of ready cash that had emboldened him to travel to Calcutta. He knew that Shivdharilal's son Shivratan lived in the city. Before leaving Chhapra, he took his address, and upon his arrival, first and foremost, reached out to him, seeking his help and counsel. Shivratan was a storekeeper at the army cantonment in Barrackpore. The two met at the cantonment storehouse. Bulakna was surprised to notice that a number of punctured drums lay abandoned at that facility. 'Good lord! What are these for?' he asked.

Shivratan explained that they were ceremonial drums used in the army bands.

'But Sir, why have they been punctured?' he asked, thoroughly puzzled.

'Fool, they have not been punctured on purpose. They are to be mended. Since we haven't found someone who can do the job, they have been temporarily stacked up in this storehouse.' Shivratan laughed at Bulakna's rustic innocence.

'You haven't found a mender in this big a city! Well, I can do this job.' Bulakna was both impressed and disappointed with Calcutta.

'In that case, show us a sample of your work? Can you mend one of these?' Shivratan dared.

Bulakna accepted the challenge. He picked up a punctured drum, and in no time, replaced the leather membrane on its batter head. By the end of that first meeting, Shivratan's fertile imagination and devious intellect had enabled him to figure out that Bulakna's pockets were indeed deep. Soon, a property was rented to open a shop and a signboard in English that read 'Bulaki Lal & Company, Musical Instrument Merchant' was promptly suspended atop its entrance. Thus, Bulakna Dom was reborn as Bulaki Lal Kayath, the sole proprietor of Bulaki Lal & Company.

They hired a manager to oversee everyday transactions at the shop, but the man was more of a dummy. The real control rested with Shivratan who made sure that the entire bulk of army's procurement of musical instruments as well as all the mending jobs were sourced from Bulakna's shop.

The little establishment was crammed with a variety of musical instruments, and before long, they started making profits. Emboldened by his gainful trade, Bulakna bought a house and married a Bengali widow.

For Mahendar, hitherto friendless in the city, Bulaki Lal & Company turned out to be a great blessing; it had brought together old acquaintances in an alien and unfriendly city. Thanks to the shop, he found a support system in the form of Bulaki Lal and Shivratan. Hereafter, he didn't have to swim all by himself in that ocean called Calcutta.

The following night, Manorama returned, too. Mahendar was ecstatic to see her and wasted no time in pouring her alcohol. But she giggled at his jaunty impatience and said, 'Misir-ji, I can't drink today. I have to go to the barracks.'

'To the barracks?'

'Yes, Misir-ji, you heard it right. To carry on with this onerous life, I need to visit the barracks. And to bear that shame, I have to drown in alcohol,' she added, wearing a forlorn smile. Mahendar wasn't sure how to console her.

Seeing him thunderstruck by the revelation, she added a note of empathy to the conversation and said, 'Misir-ji, that evening, when I first heard you sing, it felt as if I could finally find shelter in your songs; it felt as if we both were travelers from the same far-off country, trapped together in an alien city. You see, that is why I thought of befriending you. Since we haven't seen each other in the past several days, I just came over to check on you. Well then, I must go now.'

And just like that, Manorama walked away. A feeling of utter helplessness washed over Mahendar; there was nothing that he could do except look on in silent stupefaction. He experienced an odd surge of emotions—an emotion that he couldn't clearly comprehend. Perplexed, he stepped out of his room and directed his steps towards Bulaki Lal & Company.

* * *

During the months that followed, Mahendar divided his time between gate-keeping and being a complete wastrel. He started spending long purposeless hours at Bulakna's shop. And the little time he could spare at night, he reserved for Manorama. Music kept him company too. But every now and then, whenever the tunes of a poorvi struck the chord of melancholy on his heartstrings, he grew restless. During such moments, he swung between extremes: he would either drown himself in alcohol or feel completely repelled by it.

At times, feeling tormented by his circumstances, he took to desultory loitering. Every so often, as he sat watching ships recede away from Calcutta's Khirdipur dock, he thought of his own life. He felt like a ship adrift in the sea of Calcutta. And the high tide in Hooghly reminded him of his ever-swelling sorrows. It was only at the Kalibadi—

the home of goddess Kali—that he experienced a little calm. Soon, he became a regular visitor to the temple. It was the only place in the entire city which he liked visiting over and over again.

One day, as he was coming out of the Kali temple, he found himself surrounded by a horde of beggar women. In high spirits after the early-morning darshan of the goddess, he was generous with alms. After doling out the little money that he was carrying, as he tried to walk past the group, his eyes were drawn to a beggar woman who was desperately dragging forth her disabled body. Could he have known her from somewhere? Seeing her jogged his memory. By then, the woman had inched much closer. When he bent forward to take a good look at her, he glimpsed old familiar lineaments in that soiled somber face. The woman, too, appeared quite shocked. Having painstakingly dragged herself towards Mahendar, she now wanted to slink away, but she couldn't retreat at the same pace. Mahendar lunged ahead and grabbed her hand.

'Kesarbai?'

Tears rained down her eyes as she heard her name. He lifted her in his arms and to the astonishment of everyone present, set her on a carriage that was waiting nearby.

Mahendar brought her over to his place, bathed her and draped her in a new sari. Nearly half of her body was paralyzed. The queen of ambrosial melodies stuttered as she spoke. Somehow, between sobs, she managed to narrate the story of her blighted life. She had come to Calcutta with the Nawab of Banaras. During her early days in the city, life seemed heavenly. She lived in a majestic mansion, attended to by an army of underlings and guarded by gatekeepers. Her days were enveloped in splendour and life was one endless round of merrymaking, until one day she suffered an attack of paralysis. Suddenly, her sweet life was poisoned. At first, she did receive a little medical attention. However, once the nawab found another woman, she was thrown out of the mansion and forced to survive by begging near Kalibadi. Moved by her harrowing tale, Misir-ji was determined to get her cured; without any delay, she was provided with medical care.

But the medical expenses were too heavy for a gatekeeper to bear. Soon, he was forced to ask around for help, but it was not forthcoming. Manorama extended both her sympathy and support. At times, she even assisted Mahendar with nursing Kesarbai and by doing household chores. But given her meager income, and the high expenses of living in Calcutta, it was difficult for her to set aside even a small amount for Kesarbai's costly medicines. For a while, both Shivratan and Bulaki did support Mahendar with money. But one day, Shivratan spoke plainly to him and said, 'Misir-ji, there is only so much that the two of us can do. We have our own families and children to feed. If you find it so difficult to arrange for the money, why don't take to counterfeiting banknotes?'

At first, Mahendar was taken aback by the suggestion, but his desperation knew no bounds. Recovering quickly

from the initial shock, he said, 'Shivratan-ji, your
proposal is a good one. I have run into such hard times
that even counterfeiting sounds agreeable. But how do I
go about this?'

Shivratan smiled. He slid to the edge of his seat and
whispered, 'That I can teach you.'

Within a week, all the arrangements necessary for
the enterprise were made. The printing machine was
kept hidden in Manorama's room and the business of
counterfeiting was carried out only during the nights.
The room was lit by a gas lamp, dimmed to its minimal
brightness to keep the prying eyes away.

Mahendar could now afford the expensive medicines
prescribed by Kaviraj Gananath Sen for Kesarbai; paying
the hundred rupees that Sen charged was easy. In no
time, Kesarbai's health showed signs of remarkable
improvement: she could use her legs to walk and her ability
to speak improved too. To Mahendar, it was a sight that
filled his heart with joy and satisfaction. But inscrutable are
the ways of God. Kesarbai suffered a relapse so severe that
she could not be saved thereafter. In a life that oscillated
between the extremes of joy and sorrow, Kesarbai had had
the consolation of finding a little happiness before drawing
her last breath. When a grief-stricken Mahendar returned
to his room after cremating her body on the bank of the
Hooghly, Manorama came over to console him and said,
'For whom do you grieve now, Misir-ji? Those with a
desire to survive must escape the snares of the past. You

must look ahead to life, and so should I. Listen, I have saved so much that I no longer wish to continue with this dangerous trade of counterfeiting. Neither do I need to sin in the barracks, nor seek refuge in alcohol. I have used my savings to buy myself a husband. Now, I want to start my life afresh; away from Calcutta, away from these people who know my story. I'll marry and lead a respectable life. Perhaps I'll never be able to forget our time together, but at this moment, I can only seek your forgiveness.'

Manorama wasn't lying; she left Calcutta and the city became insufferable for Mahendar without her. By then, Shivratan had amassed an enormous fortune. The intriguing story of his prosperity, which had started with his partnership with Bulaki Lal & Sons, took a dramatic leap once he established his grip over the counterfeiting racket. In no time, he had become a millionaire. Meanwhile, Bulaki, too, appeared keen to take up a new enterprise. His Bengali wife, who had received a little education, had started meddling in those areas of their trade that had been left to the superior wisdom of Shivratan. Having weighed all his options, Shivratan decided to dissociate himself from both counterfeiting and Bulaki Lal's shop. He also left his job at the storehouse and secured a lucrative contract to arrange supplies for the army barracks. Soon, he opened a new firm by the name 'Munshi and Sons' in Shyambaazar and devoted himself wholeheartedly to its management. Left alone after Manorama's departure and the subsequent loss of business partners, Mahendar started reflecting on his life and circumstances. For the first time since he had come to Calcutta, he felt a little scared; he feared that his illicit trade may soon land him in jail. After all these years, he was left with nothing but the printing machine, a sense of acute bereavement at having lost Kesarbai and the lingering pain of being separated from Manorama.

All his friends in Calcutta had severed ties with their former selves. They were now absorbed into their respective new lives and trades. But Mahendar wasn't so stone-willed; the harder he tried to get away from his past, the more deeply entangled he got. His tender heart always proved a traitor. In the past, on several occasions, it had emboldened him to take a leap of faith. But just in the nick of time, it had always raised unforeseen roadblocks, causing him to stumble and fall.

When he could no longer bear living in Calcutta, he decided to go back to Mishrawaliya, his own village. The memories of the city travelled with him. He also decided on carry along two of his acquisitions from the city: his newfound fondness for alcohol to assuage his aching heart and the printing machine to keep body and soul together.

15

For your love

Mahendar returned to Mishrawaliya after ten long years. His ancestral home lay in an acute state of disrepair. Even in the olden days, his family had never seen good times. However, during those intervening years, poverty had aggravated their hardships. As soon as he reached the doorway of his old house, he was greeted by his brother; years of deprivation had reduced him to a mere skeletal frame. Those excruciating signs of scarcity—his brother's emaciated body and his ramshackle house—moved him to pity and self-loathing.

Mahendar's arrival heralded a reversal of fortunes: the house was restored, fields were tilled after long, and once more, cattle grazed on their land. Now that he had clutched a genie by its matted hair, anything seemed possible;

the machine that printed money made all his dreams come true.

Mahendar was having the time of his life. He spent his days managing affairs of the farm, while his evenings were reserved for musical gigs and get-togethers. In the middle of it all, once in a while, hundred-rupee banknotes were printed secretly in a gas lamp-lit room. At the end of each clandestine operation, the one-foot tall printing machine was shoved back in a stack of hay. The agents who took the fake banknotes to the market charged a commission of fifty rupees for every hundred they smuggled. The remainder was splurged on routine revelries and imported wine. Every night, Mahendar took to bed heavily inebriated. Yet, each dawn, he woke up dutifully to say his morning prayers and observe the rituals. Those were the bright days of abundance and hope!

One morning, as he was about to conclude his morning puja, an agent by the name Ramlal Singh appeared at his doorstep. He had brought a stranger along. Ramlal was Mahendar's most trusted accomplice; right from his early days of counterfeiting in Calcutta, He had assisted Mahendar with printing and smuggling. 'Misir Baba, this is Gopichand Sahu from Arrah. He is in the business of money-lending. I have known him for a long time, and based on that, I trust him, as much as a man trusts a member of his own family. He is very clever at exchanging bank notes. But, of late, he has fallen on hard times. If we could make use of his skills, it would be profitable for everyone involved,' said Ramlal, introducing his friend.

Mahendar narrowed his eyes and cast probing glances at Gopichand Sahu. He was rather quaintly attired; he had wrapped himself up in a frilled woollen shawl, with a soiled coarse sheet layered above it. Mahendar could not suppress his laughter.

'Well, Mr Moneylender, why do you hide your precious shawl under that dirty sheet?' asked Mahendar.

'Sir, this is the only shawl in my entire family. If this, too, were to get soiled, attending social gatherings during winters would cause a lot of embarrassment to my people.'

Mahendar found him to be an amusing person. And when he took out his betel-box to serve Magahi leaf and flavoured tobacco from Banaras, Mahendar was completely won over. After gossiping for a while, he felt confident enough to ask Gopichand pointblank, 'So, Mr Moneylender, what is the cut that you seek?'

After a brief reflection, Gopichand replied, 'Sarkar, I'll take five per hundred.'

'Only five per hundred? Well, others demand a much higher commission. Why would you settle for five?' Mahendar asked, somewhat surprised.

'Baba, didn't I tell at the very outset that I want no more than what I deserve. As you already know, I am a moneylender by trade. I can't just sit quietly atop a mound of banknotes and do nothing with them; I must lend them out to others. Such is my nature. And I cannot handle more cash than what I'll get from you; it is already too sumptuous a meal to digest, much more than I can chew. Besides, in spite of the nature of our trades, it is good to observe a little honesty. Riches amassed with cunning seldom last.'

The deal was struck. Gopichand was required to carry hundred-rupee banknotes to the market and after a few days, return with ninety-five. In no time he soared very high in Mahendar's estimation. Whenever he stopped by, he remembered to bring along Magahi betel leaves and Banarasi tobacco. Mahendar was overwhelmed with this small tribute. Gopichand was truly deft at the art of keeping one's employer happy. One day, as Mahendar was singing a poorvi song, all by himself, Gopichand joined him and started improvising on a tabla lying close at hand. That gesture had Mahendar completely floored. He thanked his stars for he had found a man so versatile and loyal. Soon, the two became intimate friends.

Having earned Mahendar's trust, Gopichand made a rather unusual request, 'Misir Baba, I am a very poor man. If you could initiate me into your secret art, I'll be forever indebted; for then, I'll be able to feed my family well.'

Mahendar readily agreed to the request, and thus, Gopichand Sahu's apprenticeship commenced. His visits became much more frequent, and whenever he came, he was showered with a lot of warmth. During the nights, when Mahendar and his brother conducted the business of counterfeiting, Gopichand stood in a corner, quietly learning the craft. Life went on as usual, until one day Gopichand caught hold of Ramlal and tried to entice him with a proposition, 'Brother Ramlal, let's just learn this art once and for all. For how much longer would we get by as mere agents? You see, Misir Baba wraps up the whole process at such a frantic speed that many of the details escape our attention. But I have a plan to buy a little extra time: if you feign diarrhea and keep running out to the fields on the pretext of relieving yourself, the interruptions will hold him up and I can use that additional time to learn the rest of the tricks. Then, the two of us can move on and launch our own business. Say, how else we can hope to provide for our families,' urged Gopichand.

Ramlal turned the idea over in his mind and agreed to the plan. That evening, as soon as the courtyard room was shut and the process of counterfeiting commenced, he dashed out to the field, leaving ajar all the doors on the way. Mahendar followed him and ensured that the doors were closed. After a while, when Ramlal returned from the field after relieving himself, Mahendar had to go out again, to let him in. Once the doors were bolted, the process recommenced. But shortly, he pretended to have another bout of diarrhea and ran out of the house carrying a mug of water. However, on this occasion, Mahendar got a little complacent and did not bother over taking the necessary precautions. Although Gopichand had shut the door of the printing room, the entrance to the courtyard remained unbolted.

A little later, when the door opened again, it wasn't Ramlal who walked in; in the blink of an eye, the room was swarmed by policemen. Mahendar was absorbed in operating the printing roller. Before he could react, he was overpowered by a burly policeman. His brother was apprehended, too. Once all the culprits were nabbed, Gopichand Sahu revealed his true identity; he wasn't Mahendar Misir's poor hireling, he was inspector Babu Jatadhari Prasad of the CID. Alas, who in this world could Mahendar Misir trust!

* * *

On the third day of his arrest, the sensational story found its way into the newspapers. It triggered a huge furore, especially across Chhapra. At the Red Mansion, Ramprakash Sahay shared the news with his grand-aunt, 'Dadi, listen to this interesting news that has appeared in today's newspaper. In Mishrawaliya, a man named Mahendar Misir has been arrested for counterfeiting banknotes. Printing equipment found to be in his possession has been seized. A CID inspector named Jatadhari, who frequented the culprit's house disguised as Gopichand Sahu, is responsible for busting the racket.'

'Apprehended who? Mahendar Misir? Mahendar Misir of Mishrawaliya?' Gulzaribai exclaimed, utterly stupefied.

The flares that always flickered secretly in her bosom had burst out as a huge conflagration. Ramprakash didn't have the faintest notion of her past. Feeling encouraged by her curiosity, he showed great keenness in reading the rest of the report out loud. But, lost in thought, she paid no attention to him. A little later, as she returned to her senses, she picked up the newspaper and started checking the details herself. Soon, her carriage was sent for, and for the first time in a long while, she drove out of the Red Mansion. Ramprakash was quite astonished at the course of events and the dramatic speed at which they had unfolded. Since the day he had arrived unannounced at the mansion, he had never seen his grand-aunt step out of the premises. He wondered as to where, after reading that piece of news, did her grandmother suddenly rush to.

But it wasn't meant to be a one-time affair; that excursion soon turned into a routine of sorts. Gulzaribai had taken it upon herself to organize Mahendar's defence. 'Advocate Sahib, I urge you to present the strongest possible defence. Come what may, Mahendar Misir must be rescued. However much money is needed, just ask me. I'll reward you with gold equal to his weight,' she appealed.

When Ramprakash heard her persuasive plea to the lawyer, he was surprised by the note of desperation in her tone. 'Who is this Mahendar Misir? But then, what does he really know about his own grand-aunt?' for the first time since his arrival, he began reflecting on these questions.

He had come to Chhapra as a ragamuffin orphan and it was Gulzaribai who had generously granted him shelter. At the start of his perilous odyssey from Gunzarawala in

Punjab, he knew precious little about the place or the whereabouts of his grand-uncle, Babu Haliwant Sahay. He had nothing but a few names to steer his journey towards a largely unknown destination; he knew of a certain Sheetlapur in Bihar, which came under the jurisdiction of Manjhi police station in Chhapra; he was aware that the said Sheetlapur was his ancestral village and that some of his blood relations still lived there; he was told that his grandfather had once visited the village in his boyhood, and later, exchanged a few letters with Haliwant Sahay. But in spite of his little knowledge of the place and its many attendant uncertainties, there was something he was absolutely sure of: he knew it for a fact that Haliwant Sahay was a prominent resident of Chhapra. It was perhaps for this very reason that his plague-stricken grandfather, alone in his deathbed after the death of his entire family, had tearfully beseeched him to seek refuge at the White Mansion.

However, no end to his miseries was in sight. At the conclusion of his onerous journey from Punjab, when he reached Chhapra, yet another misfortune awaited him; no sooner had he arrived at the Chhapra junction than he learnt of Haliwant Sahay's act of renunciation and departure from the town. Seeing him so distraught, a few sadistic reprobates had jeered at him saying, 'Dear son, don't panic. Go to the Red Mansion. There sits his concubine who has usurped all his wealth. Go, beg her for help.'

Ramprakash was so distracted that he could not get the drift of those snide remarks. When he arrived at the Red Mansion, he had found a motherly guardian in Gulzaribai, sacred as the Tulsi plant and pure as the water that flows through the Ganga-ji. Gulzaribai was equally elated to have found Ramprakash. Gradually, the responsibilities of the estate were made to rest on his inexperienced young shoulders. And, at the same staggered pace, she had started dissociating herself from the affairs of the estate. Of late, most of her time was spent inside the shrine room; she would light an incense stick and spend hours in the quiet company of the two portraits that adorned it—one of Haliwant Babu, the other of Revel Sahib. Ramprakash often saw her sitting in deep meditation.

But now, seeing her get so impatient over Mahendar Misir, he was evidently dumbfounded. He tried hard to figure out everything, but nothing made sense. What restiveness had seized his grand-aunt, he wondered. What explains her round-the-clock obsession with his court case? Who is this Mahendar Misir anyway? And what could be the true identity of his grand-aunt? The young Ramprakash felt overwhelmed by several of these puzzling questions.

Soon Mahendar Misir's trial began. Whenever he emerged from the jail complex, he would be handcuffed, surrounded by sepoys and led on by a rope tied around his waist. Inside the courtroom, as he waited in the dock, he was mostly quiet. On the days of his trial, the courtroom would be crammed with people. Gulzaribai and Ramprakash were always in attendance at his hearings. Mahendar's thick, overgrown beard contrasted handsomely with his fair complexion. Every time Gulzaribai's keen gaze lingered on his face, she felt her mind wander away into a deep reverie. Ramprakash often noticed that searching look on his grand-aunt's face.

The team of lawyers hired for Mahendar Misir's defence performed unprecedented feats of argumentative jugglery; the assignment was difficult and their endeavors were monumental. A web of arguments, comprising the most unfathomable of questions and the most outlandish of responses, was carefully woven. Every conceivable connection that could lead to a favorable verdict was greased with loads of money. The defence worked so tirelessly that Mahendar's acquittal appeared virtually assured.

But things took an unexpected turn on the big day— the day of the verdict. Mahendar stood impassively in the dock, just as on his previous hearings. And like always, nestled among the milling multitudes, Gulzaribai waited for the trial to commence. Jatadhari alias Gopichand had already submitted his deposition. The judge turned to the accused and asked, 'How do you plead to the charges alleged against you?'

When he raised his drooping head to answer, his wearied gaze fell on Gulzaribai. For a moment, their eyes met. He then turned intently to Gopichand, the betrayer. He was standing in the witness box, across the courtroom.

As he tried to remember the names and the faces of the people he had known and loved, he felt a strange stirring in his blood. In the heat of the moment, he turned towards the judge and answered without flinching, 'Indeed, Sarkar. I have been in the dirty business of counterfeiting, and I was at it when arrested.'

Gulzaribai slumped to the ground, utterly devastated. Leaning against Ramprakash, she stepped out of the courtroom and tottered to her carriage. Mahendar Misir was sentenced to ten years of rigorous imprisonment. As he was being brought out of the courtroom, chained and handcuffed, people swarmed to him from all sides. Gulzaribai closed her rheumy eyes and waited for the carriage to advance. But caught in a swirl of bereaved admirers and fascinated onlookers, her vehicle could not budge.

A little later, Gopichand came out of the courtroom. Upon seeing him, Mahendar let out a roaring laughter of disdain. Gopichand could not muster enough courage to look him in the eye; avoiding his gaze, he paced off in a different direction. Seeing him scamper away, Mahendar let out an impromptu wail.

'O' Gopichand,
You treated me to betel leaves, golden and tender,
But behold what becometh me; your love had me jailed
    forever.
O' Gopichand, your love . . .'

For a while, enraptured by his haunting song, the crowd fell silent. Gulzaribai was desperate to escape the scene, completely ruffled and struggling hard to conceal her emotions. 'Drive the carriage, hurry,' she demanded in a vexed voice. Ramprakash was still at a loss. The carriage sped off, but Mahendar's voice was still audible in the background.

Once they reached the Red Mansion, Gulzaribai flew to the shrine room and locked herself in. Fatigued by an endlessly perplexing day, Ramprakash decided to take rest on the veranda. Just then he heard a heart-rending tune of lament.

'To what avail did you print those banknotes?
O' Mahendar Misir
To what avail . . .'

He turned his ears to the source of that plaintive ballad. Yes, it was indeed coming from the shrine room. Years ago, on the banks of the river Ravi in Punjab, he had once heard a *heer*—a Punjabi folk song of love, longing and parting. But her grand-aunt's song was more haunting and grief-stricken than any tune he had ever heard before. Was it really his grand-aunt? He continued to wonder.

16

A Champak Tree for the Lovebirds

It was after many years that Lachhman Prasad of the White Mansion had walked over to Gulzaribai's home. At the gate itself he ran into Ramprakash. That chance encounter left him awestruck. Ramprasad was the spitting image of Babu Haliwant Sahay; he had the same arresting face, the same height and the same burly physique.

'Son, who are you?' he asked.

'My name is Ramprakash, sir. Babu Haliwant Sahay is my grand-uncle. My grandfather, Babu Hargovind Sahay, was his cousin.'

'And do you stay here?'

'That's right, sir.'

'Where is your father?'

'He is dead, sir,' answered Ramprakash, saddened by the question.

Prasad knew all the relatives of Babu Haliwant Sahay. He had interacted with most of them in connection with that infamous lawsuit. Yet, Babu Hargovind Sahay's name had never been broached. The mention of his name piqued his curiosity and he started probing further. When he learnt of the calamity that had befallen the boy, he was moved for a moment. However, a scheme soon took shape in his mind.

After a brief silence, he said, 'Son, go tell Bai-ji that Rai Lachhman Prasad is here.'

'Inform who, sir? My grand-aunt?'

'Grand-aunt?' At first, Prasad felt a little puzzled by the suggestion, but he was quick to gather his wits. 'Yes yes, grand-aunt,' he added. Ramprakash obliged.

Lachhman Prasad had an old axe to grind; he had planned to offer fake commiserations on Mahendar's conviction and rub salt into her wounds. For the past ten years, the Red Mansion and its residents were as good as dead to him. Gulzaribai, too, in turn, had repaid in kind by blocking him off socially; he was no longer invited to or welcomed at the Red Mansion. Naturally, she was extremely curious to find out what had brought him to her house, especially on a day like that.

Gulzaribai was affable, but guarded. She invited him to the sitting room and asked politely, 'Tell me, Rai Sahib. What can I do for you? You have but to command and I obey.'

But Prasad was busy daydreaming. He paid no attention to her. Although he had come with the sole intention to humiliate her and to vent his pent-up anger, but now that thought had somehow dissipated. Sitting in the Red Mansion, as he thought of his friend Babu Haliwant Sahay, he was consumed with remorse. However, he collected himself and greeted her back with an unexpected question, 'Bai-ji, who is this boy?'

'He is Sahib's grandson. His great grandfather was an uncle of Sahib's father. Three years ago, when he lost his family to a plague, he came to the mansion seeking refuge. He is now my grandson.'

'Bai-ji, I want your grandson.' His keen eyes lit up as he made that request.

The suggestion irked Gulzaribai greatly. 'Are you here for a laugh?' she blurted, her narrowed eyes betraying her anger.

'Bai-ji, the hair on my head has greyed. I am too old for frivolity.'

He took a pause, exhaled deeply and resumed, 'Bai-ji, truth be told; I had come here with the sole intention to cause you more hurt by talking about Mahendar Misir, and to satiate my desire for revenge. But seeing this boy, I can only think of my greying hair. I am reminded of the fact that I am a father too. My daughter, Siyasaheli, has already reached the marriageable age. Come what may, I want this boy to marry my daughter, Bai-ji.'

'What else is on your mind, Rai Sahib? Are you still working on that scheme to usurp the Red Mansion?'

perplexed by his proposition, Gulzaribai chose to speak bluntly.

'Oh! No. Not at all! You see, on the contrary. I now wish to return the White Mansion which I had grabbed through deceit,' explained Prasad, wringing his hands.

Rai Lachhman Prasad had a daughter, his only child. He wanted a *ghar-jamai*—a son-in-law who could stay with him in his house. When he saw Ramprakash, he was sure that the boy was a godsend. Considering what he was looking for, Ramprakash was indeed the most suitable match for his daughter. However, the proposal unsettled Gulzaribai.

'Rai Sahib, I have always considered myself a woman with sacred conjugal duties, and I think of Ramprakash as my own grandson. But does that change anything? To the world I am nothing but Dhelabai, the harlot. How am I supposed to have anything to do with Ramprakash's wedding?' Her voice betrayed a sad acknowledgement of a failed life.

But Prasad had a gift for getting things done his way. To escape community censure, he managed to engage Haliwant Sahay's relatives from Sheetlapur and persuaded them to take a leading part in the rituals. The tilak ceremony was organized at the Opium Bungalow in Revelgunj and it was from there that the baraat set out for Chhapra. Gulzaribai oversaw all the wedding arrangements: at times with intimate immediacy, at times with the detachment deemed necessary. Once the ceremony was over, she withdrew from everything and retreated into the shrine room.

She knew all too well what was expected of her after Ramprakash's marriage; she was neither a novice, nor a fool. She remembered everything her own mother had to contend with. Could she ever summon the same bold fortitude that Meenabai had displayed? No, without a doubt, she lacked the talent needed to lead a double life. For those reasons, she resolved to devote herself to the shrine room.

She had vivid recollections of the times when Meenabai was in the prime of youth. On countless occasions, she had seen how her mother, after a spirited performance, sobbed in private. Meenabai was that fountain of mirth which brought every mehfil to life, but deep down, she was sorrow personified. She had tried her utmost to protect Gulzaribai against the polluting touch of her trade. She had even tried to give her an education. However, when circumstances changed for the worse, she had no choice but to swallow a bitter pill and introduce her daughter to the tabooed trade—the profession of a tawaif. Later, she herself taught Gulzari the subtleties of singing and the niceties of dance.

A waiting-woman had told Gulzaribai about her mother's unfortunate journey through life. Meenabai of Muzaffarpur was in fact a resident of Lucknow. She had come to Muzaffarpur to perform at a baraat, but could never return to Lucknow. Her new city lavished on her all the luxuries of life—home, land, property, and everything else. But she never got what a woman's heart truly desires; her yearnings for someone who would shield her from the ravenous gaze of the world, as a man shields his wife, remained unfulfilled.

The waiting-woman had also told her that Meenabai wasn't in fact born in Lucknow; she had meandered into the city as a dispossessed vagrant. Back in those days, brothels were the only shelter an unguarded woman lost in an unfamiliar city could hope for. It was at one such brothel that she had learnt singing and dancing. Before long, she became so adroit at her art that she had no equal in all of Lucknow. But once fame and riches started pouring in, her profession erased her sense of selfhood; although many years went by, yet no one ever heard of the place she had come from, or of the circumstances that kept her from returning to Lucknow.

Gulzaribai was born and raised in Muzaffarpur. She truly belonged to the city, and the city belonged to her; it was here that she received a smattering of letters, and later, learnt to sing and dance; it was in the mehfils of Muzaffarpur that she unleashed the seductive force of her art. Yet, the day Ustad-ji had arrived to train her and to initiate her into that loathsome profession, Meenabai had wept her heart out. Gulzaribai could never forget that fateful day.

She also remembered the champak tree in her courtyard. Whenever it blossomed, a pair of flowerpeckers would appear out of nowhere and frolic about the laden tree. The birds were playful and twitchy, just like the young Gulzari. They flitted from flower to flower, drawing nectar with their needlelike beaks. This sprightly bustle would continue all through the day. Was Gulzaribai's own life any different? Did not she also skip from one patron to the next, plundering riches and devastating lives, as she cold-bloodedly went about her trade?

Once, in Muzaffarpur, she had caught a flowerpecker. The teensy creature was put in a bamboo cage. All through the day, Gulzari tried hard to feed it; she kept bringing fresh flowers and shoved them in through the delicate bars of the cage. However, the little prisoner was so determined to frustrate her efforts that it refused to so much as look at the flowers. By evening, having exhausted all her tricks to tame it, Gulzari surrendered to its heroic obstinacy and opened the cage. Once free, it fluttered straight to its constant companion—the one that had spent the entire day hovering noisily around the cage and presently perched wearied on a slender branch of the champak tree. Whenever she thought of that episode, a sad realization of her own solitude came to torment her.

For Gulzaribai, Muzaffarpur seemed like lost city, buried in a distant past. Yet, her childhood memories of the champak tree, and of that pair of flowerpeckers, remained clear and warm. She was so moved by the episode that to treasure its memory, she had a champak tree planted along the southern flank of her mansion. Each flowering season, the bounteous flowers of the evergreen tree welcomed several chirpy pairs of flowerpeckers.

However, she barely remembered anything of her own abduction or the other details of that fateful incident. She did recall the shining swords, but what happened after that was extremely hazy, almost dreamlike. However, Gulzaribai never forgot her maiden impression of that godly man who had welcomed her in the mansion; she always remembered his radiant complexion and his cheerful face. It was an image which Gulzaribai treasured in her heart and worshipped ever since.

In Sahay, she had found a treasure trove. The Red Mansion bestowed her with money, land, respect and fame. But that wasn't all; she discovered happiness in Sahay's friendship, learnt to be loyal, and in return, earned his trust for life. Her long-cherished desire for a man, who would protect her honor as a husband protects the honor of his wife, was also fulfilled. Later, in the twilight of her life, it was on his account that she found a loving grandnephew she could surrender all her cares to.

Yet, in spite of her little triumphs and many consolations, she had failed to keep the man all to herself. Sahay had brought her to the Red Mansion in a moment of frenzy. Back then, although he was well past his youth, he remained stubborn in his refusal to admit it. During her early days in the Red Mansion, she was the only intoxicant Sahay craved for; the sound of her anklet bells echoed in his heart, while her songs, virulent like a serpent's venom, poisoned his soul. But the period of decadence and romance was short-lived; it got jolted to a sudden end once Ramnarayan challenged Sahay's smug stupor and woke him out of his honeyed fantasy.

In that unexpected turn of events, Gulzaribai gained something priceless—something that her heart desired the most, more than all the luxuries of the world. She was accorded a form of respect that only a married woman is entitled to. Yet, in spite of everything, the aching void in her youthful heart, which desired love and intimacy, remained unfulfilled. The abyss of years which separated the two was wide and deep. Neither could Haliwant throw a bridge over that abyss, nor could Gulzaribai leap across it.

It was during those days that she had heard Mahendar Misir's voice for the first time. That day, after listening to his songs, Vidyadharibai had asked an awkwardly pointed question, 'Gulzari, why do his songs devour my heart?' Taken aback by her forthrightness, Gulzari wasn't sure of how to respond, but she knew that his songs spoke of her own agony too. It filled that void in her soul which Sahay could not.

However, Mahendar was a compulsive absconder. He always lacked patience necessary to fight adversity. In that sense, he was the very opposite of Sahay. Right through his life, Sahay had stood his ground and braved difficulties with the fortitude of a lion. Later, it was with the same defiant intrepidity that he forfeited his hard-earned wealth and embraced the life of a vagrant mendicant. He had emerged triumphant in every battle that he had fought. But Mahendar was a study in contrast. He kept fleeing from his own realities, never willing to defy the conundrums that came his way. Perhaps it was this desire to remain a perennial renegade that drove him away from Chhapra, compelling him to spend years wandering around aimlessly. It made a criminal out of him and finally, brought him to jail. Indeed, for a rolling stone like Mahendar, no place could be more secure than a jail!

Gulzaribai was shattered by the outcome of Mahendar's trial. She had always carried a torch for him. Even though they inhabited different worlds, and remained as separated as the banks of a river, yet Gulzaribai had no complaints and remained grateful for the quiet comfort that she drew from his presence. She often thought what Haliwant Babu had told her during one of their visits to Revel Sahib's grave: 'Gulzaribai, we are obligated to live our lives. And to discharge this obligation, we are expected to take up daily battles. Those who fail this sacred duty are doomed to die a thousand deaths. This is what Revel Sahib has taught me.'

But Gulzari failed to act on that wisdom; she could never really master the art of staying alive. She seesawed between feeling dead and being full of life. That day, when Haliwant Babu had suddenly walked away from her, she had felt dead. But then, she found Ramprakash, and through him, recouped her lost ardour. Later, during Mahendar's trial, she came closest to orchestrating the greatest triumph of her life. However, her finest moment was yet to come. When Prasad visited the Red Mansion, nursing an old gripe and hoping to add insult to injury after Mahendar's conviction, she surprised herself through her own capacity for empathy and forgiveness; by accepting Prasad's proposal for Ramprakash's marriage, she surrendered the only support of her old age to an ageing father's anxiety about his daughter. After that, since she had nothing more to lose, she started thinking of herself a supreme conqueror.

* * *

Life went on. A few years later, Ramprakash and his wife decided to go to Punjab. Although Ramprakash had a rewarding new life in Chhapra, he could never put Punjab out of his mind. Besides, he had inherited a little property which he wanted to sell off. Over the past few years, his fortune had swung dramatically; he had come to Chhapra a pauper, but was going back a king. When he had first met Gulzaribai, his circumstances were tragic and trying; his kith and kin were dead and the man he had come looking for had disappeared, too, having withdrawn himself from worldly concerns. But a woman—a complete stranger—had taken him under her wings, offering solace and support. As he prepared to leave, Gulzaribai wiped her tears and pleaded with the couple, 'Come back soon, son. And you, my dear daughter, take good care of him.' Ramprakash himself felt a little uneasy.

Once in Punjab, he realized that ordering the affairs of his inheritance would take longer than he had imagined. However, when Prasad wrote to him about his grand-aunt's poor health, he set all his affairs aside and rushed back to Chhapra.

Upon his return, he found the Red Mansion in a terrible state of neglect; the flower beds were covered with wild grasses and the lawn was overgrown with weeds. He panicked and hurried indoors, fearing something ominous. Gulzaribai lay on her bed; nothing but a tired skeletal frame remained of her vivacious former self. The table by her bed was loaded with bottles of medicine. Portraits of Revel Sahib and Haliwant Sahay were also made to stand on that crammed table, so that Gulzaribai may look at them all the time. They were adorned with garlands strung together with freshly plucked flowers. And a bunch of incense sticks was lit and placed next to them.

'Dadi, I am here. I have come back, Dadi. Now you will get better in no time,' his eyes brimmed over with tears as he uttered those words.

When Siyasaheli sought her blessings and touched her feet, it became impossible for Gulzaribai to restrain her emotions. However, she composed herself, wiped off her tears and said, 'I am so glad that you have come back. Now, I wish to surrender all my responsibilities to your bride and go away for good. I have no desire to get better. What is left of my duties that I would pray to God for recovery? He has already graced this sinner with everything she could have hoped for. All I want now is the chance to die in your presence, with the two of you by my side.'

She was in considerable unease and started gasping heavily once she finished the sentence. When the waiting-woman tried to give her medicine, she stopped her saying, 'No, no. Let it be. I don't need medicine anymore. My boy has come back, that is enough for me.' And then, she handed over a bunch of keys to Siyasaheli, her face exuding a profound sense of serene satisfaction.

A couple of days later, she sent for Ramprakash and made to him the most unexpected request. 'Son, I think Misir-ji's prison term is about to end. He should be released the day after tomorrow. I want you to go to Buxar and find a way to bring him here.' Ramprakash wasted no time thinking the request over and left for Buxar at once.

As Mahendar emerged from the precincts of the Buxar jail, he found Ramprakash waiting for him. He had no difficulty recognizing Ramprakash. During the trial, he had seen him on several occasions, accompanying Gulzaribai in the courtroom. Ramprakash pressed his hand and pleaded, 'Misir-ji, come, let us go.'

Mahendar left for Chhapra in the company of Ramprakash, his mind crowded with troubled thoughts. When they reached the Red Mansion, a crowd awaited them at the gate. Prasad was also there.

'How is my Dadi?' Ramprakash inquired nervously.

'What shall I say, son. Perhaps she wants to look at you once more, before breathing her last,' Prasad replied in a somber tone.

The river Saryu was in spate. Whipped by its strong waves, the southern wall of the campus had collapsed. The river had burst its bank and flowed into the premises, forming a pool in the lawn. Ramprakash grabbed Mahendar's arm and took him to Gulzaribai's room. Siyasaheli was standing by her bed, holding a bowl of the sacred water from the Ganga-ji. Pataluwa and Jiriya had also come; they stood motionless in a corner of the room, sniffling intermittently. Grief weighed everyone down.

'Have you come, my boy? Misir-ji, you too! Oh, I am such a fortunate woman.'

She took a pause, drew a long breath and spoke to Mahendar, her voice barely audible, 'Misir-ji, I have lived my life, as lives are meant to be lived. My end draws near. I hope to be as brave when death comes for me. Your songs have taught me so much about being alive. I wish to listen to one last song before I die. Please, sing for me, the last song of my life.'

Her request moved everyone to tears. Mahendar was dumbstruck. 'Misir-ji, there is no time to weep and wail. Pray, hurry. Sing me that last song.' Although her sweet ringing voice of yesteryear had dropped to a feeble whisper, her tone was still decorous.

Mahendar Misir did as she said. Almost unthinkingly, a song flowed from his lips.

'O blessed bride,
I see a fair, in the city of snares
O blessed bride,
Fineries are sold, precious and rare . . .'

Throughout the song, Gulzaribai wore a gentle smile on her face, and her weary eyes remained riveted to Sahay's portrait. Once the song ended, people realized that she had departed for her heavenly abode. Letting out a loud wail, Ramprakash collapsed at her feet. Everyone present burst into tears. Leaning against the door, Lachhman Prasad sobbed too. It seemed as though the Saryu herself streamed down his eyes. It was all over.

A ferocious wave had forced its way into the lawn and swept off the champak tree. The phoolsunghi that lived on the tree hastily flew away.

Glossary

Tawaif: loosely, a nautch girl; a courtesan accomplished in dance, music, poetry and etiquettes; embodies cultural sophistication.

Baraat: a groom's marriage procession; in Bihar, the emphasis is more on pageantry than on procession; often associated with colourful marquee and nautch.

Poorvi: literally 'of the east', refers to both Bhojpuri songs and Hindustani classical tunes; Mahendar Misir is considered its greatest proponent in Bihar.

Birahin: Bhojpuri folk songs of love-in-separation; often addressed to an absent husband who toils away in a faraway city.

Kathak: an Indian classical dance form associated with the story tellers of north India and Mughal courts.

Kotwal: police officer in colonial India; as the immediate representative of a distant government, a source of disciplining terror in rural areas.

Sarkar: an administrative dispensation, in rural parlance, a gender-neutral term that refers to someone in a position authority; someone people supplicate to.

Aanchal: the flowing end of a sari, linked with modesty as it is used by women to cover their head; in popular imagination, a metaphor for a woman's affection.

Khoencha: an auspicious gift of rice, vermillion, money, etc. bundled in aanchal or a piece of cloth; generally given when a married woman is about to embark on a journey.

Mujra: a soirée centred on a tawaif, meant for male patricians and held inside a nautch house; involves singing, dance routines, poetry recitation etc.

Mehfil: a festive gathering, necessarily with a musical performance, preferably with dance recitals, too; sometime involves drinking.

Darshan: the ritual of beholding the face of deity; ideally, in a manner that the eyes of the idol meet those of the devotee.

Thumri: North Indian classical songs, combines romantic and devotional sentiments; usually rendered in a feminine voice; associated with the court of Wajid Ali Shah in nineteenth century Lucknow.

Dadar: North Indian semi-classical vocal style; draws upon folk and household themes, sung by women.

Tappa: North Indian folk songs.

Ji: a common gender-neutral honorific, suffixed to a name

Bai: an honorific for Indian women; in Hindi heartland, suffixed to a tawaif's name; Bai-ji is a common double honorific for tawaifs.

Baba: a form of salutation suffixed to someone's name; reserved for monks, elderly, experienced and Brahmins.

Ustaad: a maestro or an expert; in the Indian subcontinent, refers to a highly skilled musician or an connoisseur of wrestling.

Acknowledgements

Translating *Phoolsunghi* made me realize the ethos of the vernacular cultures. This wasn't just another academic exercise, of the kind where a scholar indulges in a dreary, solitary pursuit, vying for recognition from peers; it brought a community of Bhojpuri enthusiasts together, making the project a truly collective enterprise.

I feel a deep sense of gratitude to the late author's family—his wife Susheela Pandey, his daughter Ambuja Sinha and his son-in-law, Rajeshwar Prasad Sinha—for sharing their insights into his craft, and also books from his vast collection. Vinay Mishra, Mahendar Misir's great grandson, was forthcoming with facts, documents and anecdotes about his illustrious ancestor. I am truly indebted to Dr Munna Pandey who put his own copy of the book into my hands, prodding me constantly to translate it. Dr Brijbhushan Mishra, a doyen of Bhojpuri literature, was patient with all my queries, and allowed me to lean on his scholarship. I benefited greatly from the pioneering work done by Vishwanath Sharma, Ranjan Vikas and Ranjan Prakash—three dedicated bibliophiles—who have put together a sizeable library of Bhojpuri works. Gratitude is also due to Anand-ji, the translator of several Hindi classics, for alerting me to the errors of my style. I have to thank Chandrahas Choudhury, who volunteered to look into my draft and shared valuable inputs. My long conversations with Dharmendra Sushant, easily one of the best scholars of Bhojpuri and everything else, shaped my introduction, in ways only the two of us can understand. With Animesh Mohapatra and Lalit Kumar, my oldest allies in the city, I exchanged daily notes on the progress of translation, reading out each chapter to them as soon as it was rendered into English. This translation would not have been possible without inputs from Prof Devendra Choubey, Dr. Prithviraj Singh, Dr Bhagwatiprasad Dwivedi, Dr Jaikant Singh, Dr. Santosh Patel, Prof. Jyotirmaya Tripathy, Dr Baidik Bhattacharya, Dr V.M. Jha, Dr T.N. Ojha, S.N. Dubey, Mihir Jha, Dr I.M. Jha, Dr Dilip Choubey and Dr G.K. Jha, the principal of my college. Sashwat Panda, a young scholar with remarkable perspicacity, helped wholeheartedly with revision. I wish to thank my friends—Prabhat Ranjan, Abhaas, Chandrima Chatterjee, Umashankar Patra and Aruni Mahapatra—for all the support and help they have extended. My brother Pankaj Chaubey, Rajeev Pathak,

Pawan Chaturvedi, Namrata Chaubey, Vidhshree, Indrajeet Jha, Khushboo and Anushri, with their deep interest in folk cultures kept me motivated, reminding me constantly of the significance of this project. I was extremely fortunate to have Ananya Bhatia as my editor; her enlightened approach to translation as well as her work ethics, both deserve special praise. Rajnikant Pathak, Neeta Pathak and Aadya Pathak— my family in Patna—helped me procure books, documents and prioritised my engagements whenever I happened to be in the city. Prabhas Upadhyay, Asha Upadhyay and Divyani showered much warmth and care during this past winter, as I sat in their quiet sunbathed garden, finalizing the first draft of the manuscript. I wish to thank my father, Madhusudan Choubey, for being who he is—understanding, compassionate and protective. My wife, Indrani Nilima, deserves to be thanked for stepping into multiple roles for my sake, all very different and demanding. She shared my fatigue, frustrations and exhilaration, right from the afternoon I translated the first page of *Phoolsunghi*. Finally, I can't help thinking of my mother, who was responsible for my earliest encounter with Bhojpuri literature; years ago, she read out to me a short story in Bhojpuri, which was written by her father.

Gautam Choubey
Mayur Vihar, New Delhi
27 September 2020